"LYDIA THORNE IS DEAD."

I groaned. "Let me guess. She was found in her cabin with a knife in her back, while her faithful white horse grazed outside. The groom said the only visitor was one private detective, Abbie Doyle. Am I right so far?"

She nodded. "On the money. You had access. You disappeared into the woods with her. You returned alone pretty winded. You wanted to talk with her, but when you returned, you told the groom you'd lost her in the woods."

Standish stood up and glared at me. "I have one question to ask. Did you murder Mrs. Thorne?"

————————— ★ —————————

Anna Ashwood Collins

Deadly Resolutions

WORLDWIDE®

TORONTO • NEW YORK • LONDON
AMSTERDAM • PARIS • SYDNEY • HAMBURG
STOCKHOLM • ATHENS • TOKYO • MILAN
MADRID • WARSAW • BUDAPEST • AUCKLAND

DEADLY RESOLUTIONS

A Worldwide Mystery/April 1994

This edition is reprinted by arrangement with
Walker and Company.

ISBN 0-373-28015-7

In memory of my late husband,
George W. Collins

ONE

ROTTEN THINGS HAPPEN to me when it rains. I wrecked my car a couple of years ago, I broke my ankle in a rainstorm at Chincoteague, I found Mize's body in a storm just like this one.

The rain blotted out all in existence except for the little wet box it made around my body. Water streamed off my felt fishing hat, ran down my neck, dripped from my nose and chin. My pants stuck to my skin, cold and clammy. Water from my jacket oozed down my tailbone. I have been wetter, but I don't remember when.

We were a miserable but dedicated little group, the New York Coast Walkers. We were concerned about our marine environment. The parent organization, National Marine Environment Association, met once a year to discuss priorities and set policy. The New York group—the most active one, followed by the locals in San Diego and Tampa—concentrated on New York, New Jersey, New England, and the Chesapeake Bay area. Along with the serious business of preserving the marine environment, we also believed in having fun.

Every New Year's Day, we walked the beach at Breeze Point, part of Gateway National Park on the Rockaway Peninsula in Queens. Today, only six intrepid members, four women and two men, had appeared at the office building on Fort Tilden, now part of the park.

The ranger sipping coffee in his office had looked at us as if we were balmy. He was right. Nobody wanted to chicken out, so nobody suggested the better part of sanity might be to adjourn to the meeting room, drink a little wine, and watch slides. So, here we were, slogging in the rain.

Trudging along, head down, I bumped into one of the group. They were staring out to sea where a sea gull, desperately flapping its wings, was being swept under by each successive wave.

"That bird's in trouble," Mary Ann, our resident kind heart, yelled above the wind.

I, Abigail Doyle, not being a sea gull lover, shrugged. But Ricky Carter, our group leader, a feisty, skinny fellow in his fifties and an Audubon member, waded into the water and captured the bird. The bird bit him. Ricky didn't seem to mind as he cradled it to his chest.

"A young bird. Winter's been hard on him. I don't think he'll make it," he said. Ricky rubbed the bird's head and whispered to it while the rest of us shifted from foot to foot, huddling deeper into our wet clothes, wishing Ricky would get on with wringing its neck or whatever he was going to do with it. He gently placed the bird in the lee of a cement slab left over from World War II coastal defenses.

The bird glared at me. How did it know I was the only sea gull hater in the crowd? "So long, bird," I muttered as I plodded after the group. "Anyone for a cup of coffee?" I yelled. They ignored me.

When I caught up, they were gathered around Jill, our plant maven, listening to her expound on a piece of seaweed. Ricky nudged my arm and pointed. I glanced ahead.

"Hey, that looks like an old bunker. Let's explore it," I said. I'm not a war buff, but I figured it would be dry and shelter us from the wind for a while.

Stumbling through the wet clinging brush, we cautiously approached the half-open door. Muggers, winos, crack heads, assorted derelicts, vandals, and teenage lovers regularly used these bunkers. We crowded into the entrance where we stopped to listen. Silence. Light from the partially open doors at each end of the bunker cast a ghostly illumination, just enough to discern shadows. Two darkened squares on one side of the passage appeared to be entrances to side rooms.

I wrinkled my nose at the reek of urine, decay, and something else that was vaguely familiar but escaped me at that moment. It was a relief to be out of the wind.

"Here's a candle," Jill said, stooping down to pick it up. "Anybody got a match?"

We laughed. "Clean-living bunch," I said, "no smokers." At that moment not smoking seemed like a terrible disadvantage.

Bob edged his way into one of the dark passages. Mary Ann said, "I wouldn't go in there. Probably full of rats."

"Rats!" someone yelped as we all scuttled toward the entrance.

As he turned to follow us, Bob tripped. "Damn. There's something here."

We waited.

"It's a—a body."

Silence. I considered Bob's announcement. Maybe I should explain that I'm no stranger to bodies, dead or alive. My card says I'm an efficiency expert, but that's just a polite way of saying if you have a tricky problem, I'll solve it. Sometimes those problems involved dead bodies.

I'm an expensive private detective who refuses to acknowledge that as my primary occupation, and I am very selective in my clientele, most of whom come to me via my business consultations. Since I design systems for factories, business and institutions, I'm always meeting a socially elite group. Even they have tiresome problems such as robbery and murder.

Probably some poor wino who froze to death, I thought as I joined Bob. I prodded the body with my foot. I knelt, felt for the arm, noted the body was still slightly warm, found the wrist, checked the pulse, followed the arm up to the neck, checked again for a pulse.

"Dead all right," I said. Lightly frisking the upper body, I touched some cold metal on the chest and fingered them. Military medals?

I stood up. "Go back to the office and call the police. I'll stay here." Despite a few halfhearted protests, they gladly fled.

I watched from the doorway until they disappeared into the mist. Turning around, I accidentally kicked the candle that Jill had dropped, then picked it up. I searched the victim's pockets where I found a lighter.

"Eureka! Let there be light."

I stared at the body, stunned. I'd never seen a dead general before—Corps of Engineers castle insignia, two shiny stars—a major general, with medals all over his chest and a neat bullet hole in his heart. Bullet hole! We should have heard a shot. I sniffed. Of course, that elusive scent had been cordite. Smells linger on damp air.

I smiled grimly. The only times I associated with Corps officers were during public hearings when our group was protesting or testifying against some project that promised to destroy even more of our marine environment. Those brass types were always so pompous, armored in their tailored uniforms and armed with impressive folders full of colored graphs and interminable figures. A friend of mine, a major in Army Intelligence, sneered at engineers, lawyers, and doctors as civilians in uniform—not true-blue military people.

"Well, here's one who won't be destroying any more wetlands," I muttered as I studied his face. I have an excellent memory for faces and his didn't ring a bell.

Something bothered me. I rocked back and forth on my heels while I pondered. Of course! His uniform was dry. It had been raining for hours. Did he come here during the night to meet somebody? Early this morning? Why the uniform? Doesn't make sense. I shivered. Then again, maybe he was on his way to the Army Reserve center down the street.

I checked for identification. No wallet. There was a slightly faded mark on the jacket where a name tag had been before he or someone else removed it. Using the candle, I scanned the immediate area. Found a spent shell casing a few feet away. Left it. I studied the soles of his shoes. Dry. A piece of bayberry clung to his left lower pant leg. That came from the inland side, I thought, not recalling any bayberry shrubs between the beach and the bunker. I stared at the body. That's how I work. I stare until something comes to me. Unfortunately, nothing came.

A siren penetrated my reverie. "They're awfully close. Must be some kind of road near here." Another habit. I talk to myself. I doused the candle and moved to the door. The siren stopped, doors slammed, voices rose and fell as they neared the bunker. Ricky was leading, followed by a tall slender woman I had never seen before. Detective, I guessed. Times sure have changed.

Ricky ducked inside and shook the rain off his hat. "Detective Standish, Abby Doyle, one of our members."

I looked up, then some more. She was at least six feet four inches tall. No slouch either. Proud of her height. Shoulder-length red hair framed a stern but attractive face. Somehow, I didn't think she was the type of woman you called Red. Her eyes were green—cynical cat's eyes that discouraged easy familiarity. They narrowed as she stared at me. I figured she had neat slots for everybody and she had just filed me under middle-aged busybody.

She flicked on a large flashlight. "Where's the body?"

"In here," I said, seeing the general clearly for the first time as she played the light on his body. He was older than he had looked in candlelight.

"Did you touch anything?"

"No. I checked his pulse. We had no light." I crossed my fingers behind my back, conscious of the candle in my pocket, and shivered again from the damp cold.

She glanced at me. "Go sit in my car before you catch pneumonia. The rest can leave. I want their names, phone numbers, and addresses. I'll get in touch with them later."

"Can't I go too? I'm freezing. I'd like to get out of these wet clothes."

"I want to talk to you. It's nice and warm in my car. You can listen to the police calls."

I smiled wanly, detecting her note of sarcasm. She was about as subtle as a sledgehammer.

After Ricky handed her a list of names, the group piled into his station wagon and left. I enjoyed the car's heat. While I waited for Detective Standish to begin her third degree, she was drumming her fingers on the steering wheel and humming tunelessly.

"You know," she finally said, "I have this annoying trait. I never forget a name. Abby Doyle. Now, where do I know that name from?"

"Donation list for the Police Athletic League?" I asked.

"Diamonds? Yes, diamonds. The movie star—what's her name...?"

"Laura Monteith?"

"Right. Her diamonds were stolen from her room in the Plaza. She politely told the police to buzz off and hired someone to recover her jewels. An efficiency expert. I thought it peculiar at the time. What could an efficiency expert know about police work? I filed the name. Doyle. Abigail." She turned her head and glared at me. "Now, tell me what you're really doing here."

I sighed. "Taking the annual New Year's Day walk with the New York Coast Walkers."

"In the pouring rain?" she scoffed. "So you could lead them to a still-warm body?"

"Are you insinuating I knocked off that general? How melodramatic."

"I suspect somebody in your charming little group of oddballs did exactly that."

"Oddballs?"

"What else would you call a bunch of nuts out walking around in weather like this? New Year's Day is for recovering, for football, for eating, for sleeping—not for walking around in the freezing rain, finding dead generals in old bunkers—"

"Don't you think you're a little overwrought?"

She exhaled noisily. "I hate amateurs. Just remember that, Doyle. You can go. I'll call you if I need you."

"You're tossing me out in the cold rain? You're not going to give me a ride back to the barracks?"

"Sorry, Doyle, can't leave the body alone. Just follow the road." She smirked. "You can't get any wetter. Remember, you and your buddies like water."

I climbed out slowly, giving her a real hangdog look. "If I catch pneumonia, it'll be your fault," I muttered.

"I have the feeling if you catch pneumonia, it'll be my lucky day." She reached across and slammed the door in my face. I vowed to remember the sadistic grin on her face. As my mother used to say, "It's a long road without a turning."

I plodded through the rain, wondering how I could turn a profit from a dead general. Efficiently, of course. Solving crimes was a profitable and entertain-

ing hobby, especially since most of my business involved prosaic activities such as designing more
productive assembly lines and streamlining business
operations.

The gang was waiting in the barracks meeting room,
sipping hot coffee and munching donuts. They hailed
me when I oozed through the door. I managed a halfhearted smile. "Ricky, did you recognize that general?"

Ricky stroked his beard. "Nope. Did you?" His
gaze darted around the room.

I shook my head. "Can't be a lot of generals in New
York. Anybody dealt with the Corps lately?" In our
kind of organization someone's always protesting a
Corps project.

Jill said, "Maybell Peters is in charge of Corps
protests, but she's in Florida for the winter."

"No doubt there's more to protest down there," I
said dryly as I shed my sopping jacket and wondered
about the propriety of shedding my saturated pants as
well. "Anybody hear anything that sounded like a
shot or a car motor when we were walking on the
beach?"

"In that wind, who could hear anything?" Mary
Ann said as she handed me a cup of coffee.

My little group of oddballs, I thought. Suspects?
Mary Ann Morris, high-school art teacher. Ricky
Carter, stock analyst who envisaged himself as Ranger
Rick. Jill Withers, housewife and mother of six, a
frustrated botanist. Bob Amato, furniture salesman at

Macy's, and an avid fisherman. Debbie Krupp, junior marine-science major. Hardly anyone who'd appear on the FBI's Ten Most Wanted List; I hoped Standish wasted her time chasing them down.

To make some capital out of the general's death, I had to identify him before the police did. Since they had access to national fingerprint records, that didn't give me much of a head start.

"Does anyone have a friend in the Corps?" I asked.

Silence. That was like asking the Raiders if they fraternized with the Steelers. Finally, Debbie shuffled her feet and, with blushing guilt, admitted, "Well, I did date one once." Everyone stared at her. "I went to school with him, before he was in the Army," she added defensively.

"Where is he now?" I asked.

"Right here in New York. His family lives next door to mine." She shrugged. "So—all right, I had a date with him last night. He hasn't dug up any salt marshes or built any dams yet."

We laughed at her discomfort.

"Call him. Tell him I want to ask him a question." I waited impatiently while she whispered to her friend. Finally, she handed me the phone. "My name is Abby Doyle and I need some information in a hurry." That didn't sound too cool so I tried again. "I met a Corps general at a party last night and said I'd call him today, but I've lost the paper with his name and address." I giggled, giving him the impression of a flighty little woman; then I described my general.

"That sounds like General Thorne. Begging your pardon, ma'am, if you're a member of Debbie's group, he's not the kind of man you'd want to get mixed up with. He hates all the conservationists. He'd dam up the Hudson and East rivers and turn Manhattan into a reservoir, if he could."

"Sounds charming. Where does he live?"

"Somewhere on Long Island. Could I speak to Debbie now?"

I relayed the information to the group, adding, "When Standish finds out about him we'll all become prime suspects. We've had a lot of dealings with the Corps and none of them good. Fortunately, I don't think any of us have dealt with this guy directly. Right?" I paused as I looked directly at each one of them. Nobody admitted knowing our dead general. "Anybody got a skeleton in his or her closet?"

Ricky rubbed his beard, his small brown eyes looking worried. "Finch, Cochran and Case is a very stuffy firm. I don't think my boss would appreciate my being investigated for murder."

As I listened to Ricky I thought of something I wanted to ask him, but Jill distracted me when she laughed and said, "My kids would be thrilled. They think Mom is a pretty dull dog."

"My kids will be thrilled too, but the board of ed can be a little stuffy," Mary Ann said.

Bob shrugged. "I'm sure Macy's has other employees who've been investigated for crimes. She couldn't seriously suspect any of us, could she?"

"She'd suspect her own mother if she found her at the scene of a murder," I said as I looked at Debbie, dreamy-eyed and still whispering to her friend. A star-crossed romance if I ever saw one, unless the younger breed in the Corps was more tolerant and conscious than their predecessors of the environmental disaster the human race was creating.

"I figure we've got twenty-four hours before Standish gets desperate and starts on us. Debbie, hang up." I waited until she finished her lingering good-bye. "Debbie, go home and talk to your friend. Find out all he knows about this Thorne, then leave a message on my answering machine. Jill, you're in charge of finding out where he lives. If you have to, call every Thorne on Long Island and ask for the general. Ricky, check your financial connections and see if there's any major project in the works in this area. Bob and Mary Ann, come with me. Bob and I will distract Standish while you take a good look at the general's face. We need a sketch. Any questions?"

Sirens whined in the distance. "Here comes the ambulance. Hurry." We jumped into Bob's car and raced back to the bunker.

Standish was waiting with the general. Her large flashlight hung on a spike, illuminating the body and the surrounding area. When we entered, she groaned, "What do you jokers want now?"

I sidled closer to the body. Mary Ann edged up near my shoulder while Bob moved to the other side of the detective.

"We thought you might be lonely." I smiled.

Standish glanced at Bob before she focused suspiciously upon me. "You guys up to something? Is there something you want to tell me about our friend here?" She gestured at the body.

I peeked at Mary Ann, who was concentrating on the general's face. She winked at me.

"Sounds like the rest of your crew coming," I said. "Well, see you around, Detective Standish. If you need any help, just call."

She glared at us. "You bet you jokers will see me around. Beat it."

We didn't need a second invitation. Outside, the rain was easing. "Now it stops," Mary Ann said, "now that our walk is over."

To some people beach walks are more important than dead generals.

"Can you give me a reasonable facsimile of his face?" I asked.

"No big deal. Bushy eyebrows, prominent forehead, thin nose, thin lips, overall mean look, slight scar near the left ear running vertically down the jawbone, blue eyes, black hair streaked with gray, strong jawline. Did I miss anything?"

I looked at her in amazement. "Terrific word picture, but can you draw him?"

"Let's go back to my car and we'll see. I always carry a sketch pad."

Two blue-and-whites and an ambulance crowded us off the narrow pavement. Bob's car lurched to a stop.

"Damn cowboys," he shouted. "Come on, Abby, you and I can push while Mary Ann drives."

"Why can't I drive and Mary Ann push?"

He gave me a disgusted look. "You're bigger."

We heaved the car back onto the road.

Bob and I sat in the back seat of Mary Ann's car so we could look over her shoulder. With a few deft strokes of her pen, a likeness of the general grew on the paper.

Bob grinned. "Just like one of those police artists."

Mary Ann displayed the finished drawing. "What do you think? Have I got him?"

I studied it. "Maybe a little less flare to the nose."

"Nitpicking. You know I've got him," she said cockily.

"Right. Just kidding. Hustle it over to Debbie's and have her soldier boy look at it, just to make sure it's Thorne. Then get fifty copies made at one of those quick copy places."

"On New Year's Day?"

"Oh, hell, forget the copies. Come to my place after you see Debbie's friend and we'll make plans."

TWO

Friday Afternoon

A GRATEFUL BUSINESSMAN had renovated the top floor of his Long Island City factory and given it to me rent-free for twenty-five years as part of my fee after I had figured out how to make his obsolete factory productive without spending a fortune on renovations.

The building was across the street from a rubble-strewn abandoned railroad right-of-way on the bank of the East River. The area was seedy and decaying, but I had terrific views of the Manhattan skyline.

I loved to watch the shipping traffic on the river. However I could have done without the constant buzzing of the helicopters racing back and forth from Manhattan to LaGuardia and Kennedy airports.

On weekends, holidays, and evenings, the area was quiet, practically deserted except for the patrons of a couple of seafood restaurants down the street.

The railroad right-of-way ran a few blocks inland from the river. There was a small business district on Fifth Street. St. Mary's Church, Convent, and School anchored one end of the neighborhood. The area reminded me of a small western town with its one- and two-storied buildings and small bars, restaurants, barbershops, hardware stores, fruit stands, and offices at street level.

The neighborhood encompassed both extremes common to cities: neat restored homes, and littered abandoned lots and rotting factories. A community in transition, but which way was it going? It had two things in its favor—those terrific views of Manhattan and convenient transportation. Nearby was the entrance to the Midtown Tunnel with its service tower dominating the neighborhood. Or you could catch the Number 7 subway line for a short hop into Grand Central Station or Times Square.

I glanced toward Manhattan before I pulled my rented car into the narrow alley. I never tired of looking at the skyline. So unreal. A theatrical backdrop. Today, the mist sawed off the tops of the buildings.

To reach my apartment, I took a freight elevator that fronted on the alley. When I opened the door to my apartment, the heat felt terrific. I stripped and headed for the shower.

I need an indoor hobby, I thought as I let lukewarm water stream off my back. I hate hot showers; they're bad for the heart. The black and red bathrobe cheered me up. My favorite colors. I rubbed the steam off the mirror to see how badly I'd shriveled up.

Hazel eyes under black arched brows gazed back at me. Cynical lips twitched, emphasizing the deep smile marks. I was a nervous smiler. Straight nose and high cheekbones were a legacy of my Iroquois ancestors. Damp, short curly hair tumbled over my forehead.

Not beautiful, but interesting, most people said. I was forty and could have passed for... well, forty.

I stretched aching muscles and hoped I wasn't coming down with a cold. Slipping on a robe, I headed for the kitchen, made it halfway before the secret doorbell rang. Only people I trusted knew about the concealed button near the elevator. Using the other obvious button alerted me that a stranger was at my door. I pressed the switch that opened the elevator door and activated its controls.

Mary Ann skipped across the empty hall. "Boy, this place always fascinates me. You were lucky to find it."

"It found me." I noticed she was still wet. "You didn't take time to go home?" She shook her head. "Wait." I got her one of my terry robes. "Take a hot shower. I'll toss our wet clothes into the dryer and make some coffee."

After we'd settled in the living room with a misty view of Manhattan, I studied the drawing of Thorne. "So, it was him. I wish Jill would call. Did Debbie's friend have anything to add?"

Mary Ann sighed. "Ah, this is luxury. To be warm and dry and have that splendid view. I'd like to paint it someday."

"Forget the view."

"Oh, Debbie's friend. I showed him the picture. He said it was Thorne. Debbie, smart girl, hadn't mentioned he was dead. Her young man, John, nice fellow for a digger, said this Thorne isn't too popular. He's not really assigned to the New York district.

Washington, Pentagon, John thinks. Thorne doesn't say much to the local boys. His excuse for being around so much is that his family lives on the Island."

I interrupted. "You mean he's been hanging around the local office?"

"Well, yes and no. He's been in there, but at odd hours, when the district commander is home or out of town. He bullies the underlings. John says he's always pawing through various files."

"He's been skulking around New York and his warm body turns up in a bunker. Interesting. Who profits? *Cherchez le dollar*."

"What happened to the woman?"

"That's for detective stories."

While I made sandwiches, Mary Ann said, "Let me call my husband in case he looked up from a bowl game and missed me."

WE SAT in companionable silence watching the afternoon slip away. The mist cleared and the clouds parted just at sunset. The sun slipped through the clouds and backlit Manhattan in a fiery red.

Mary Ann brushed tears from her eyes. "It's so beautiful. You've got to let me set my easel up here some afternoon like this."

"Only if I get the painting."

She scanned my collection of prints and paintings hanging on almost all of the available wall space—everything from Miró prints to Lizzul seascapes.

"Where would you hang it?"

"Just paint it. I'll make room." I glanced at my watch. "I feel useless, just sitting here, watching the sun set. Wonder how the others are doing."

The phone rang. Before I could even say hello, Ricky blurted, "Ever hear of LaChance Construction? They have everything set to build a seven-hundred-unit condominium plus marina in a Jersey marsh. All they lack is a Corps permit to dredge and fill in the wetlands."

I turned the computer loose. "Let me guess. Someone from LaChance has been in contact with our general. Wonder what the fee was to be—money now or a cushy job after retirement? Who owns LaChance? How come we haven't heard anything about this project in our organization? Shouldn't there be hearings or something? How far along is the planning?"

"I'm in the office now, looking for answers to all those questions. I know we haven't had any reports to our chapter. Maybe the national organization has something. As for ownership, it's another one of those companies that uses mirrors to conceal the real owners. Layers upon layers. Holding companies, the usual thing. It will take a while to unravel it. I'll get back to you."

"Thanks, Ricky. You're doing great." I filled Mary Ann in on the latest information.

"What do we do now?" she asked.

I smiled. "You go home. I have some serious thinking to do."

Mary Ann emerged from the laundry room, holding a lighter in her hand. "Thought you didn't smoke. Found this in your pants pocket."

I took it, turned it over and over in my hand. Fancy. Gold. Initial J. "What's Thorne's first name?"

"Martin, I think. Where'd you get the lighter?"

"From his pocket. In the excitement, I forgot to put it back." I tossed it up and down. "Now, how do I get it back to the police?"

"What's his wife's first name?" Mary Ann asked.

I shrugged. "What difference does it make?"

"Women usually use their first initials in monograms, because their last names are subject to change. Men traditionally use their last initials."

I stared at her. "I never knew that. I'm not a great monogram buyer. I'd probably pick up either one. But if his wife's name isn't Joan or something, we have an added starter, don't we?"

I flicked on the outside television camera that scanned the alley, part of my technology that made living in this type of area safer. It also saved me from unpleasant surprises or unwanted visitors.

"Looks quiet out there." I patted Mary Ann on the shoulder. "You did a super job. Keep in touch."

THREE

I STARED AT the lights of Manhattan for a long time. A lot of people lived over there with nothing more interesting to look at than the Queens skyline. Sure, Sutton Place was a classier address than Long Island City, but I was happy here. No neighbors, no distractions, just a distant hum of machines during the week. But then, my apartment was so soundproof that I was really feeling, more than hearing, a hum.

Unfortunately, the greedy politicians and their real-estate buddies in Manhattan were casting covetous glances at the Long Island City shoreline, envisioning towering apartment complexes for the rich with stunning views of Manhattan and a neighborhood gentrified with precious little boutiques and quiche restaurants. The factories, the row houses, the old stores, the shabby empty lots would have to go. I'd have to go; my factory home would be demolished. And there'd be no place in those fancy co-ops for someone who delved into seedy incidents, even if they were the seedy incidents of the rich. On the plus side, government moved slowly, so I had a few years left. Hopefully, they'd reclaim all of Manhattan's decaying shoreline before they got around to Queens.

While I had been contemplating the view, my brain had sifted through the facts. I sighed. I had to return to that bunker tonight.

THERMAL UNDERWEAR topped by black shades, a heavy sweater, dark green hunting boots, and a black watch hat turned me into a warm shadow. I slipped a rapier-thin knife into my boot sheath. I hefted a small automatic before I returned it to the drawer. I had a license to carry a gun, but didn't often bother. Guns are more apt to kill the carrier than the assailant. Besides, a knife was silent, and symbolic of my Indian heritage.

The night was cloudy and windy. Traffic was light. Most people were home watching football games or recovering from last night's excesses. I parked my car at the entrance to a shuttered beach colony a half mile beyond the bunker.

Using my small flashlight, I picked my way down the beach. No lights where I estimated the bunker to be meant the police weren't around. I looked for the cement slab where we had left the sea gull. The light reflected off a glowing eye. The gull glared at me. "Still with us, eh," I muttered as I paused to listen. The surf roared. The wind howled.

There's something eerie about being alone at a murder scene, especially in a dark, desolate area. All my senses were painfully acute. I sniffed the rankness of rotting seaweed, tasted salt on my lips, and heard the skeleton-like clicks of bayberry bushes. My skin crawled; I felt something alien. Slowly, I walked inland toward the bunker.

At first, I thought I was imagining things. Just ahead of me something growled. What had one of the men said this afternoon? Something about a pack of wild dogs? Oh, yes, Bob had said the dogs would get the gull before the night was over. Another growl, a rustling sound. Something was skulking through the bushes in front of me.

Man has an inborn fear of wolves going back to caveman days when he must have huddled in his cave listening to those bloodcurdling howls of the kings of the night. Modern man and woman have the same fear of dog packs.

Dog packs were inevitable in a city that had millions of pet dogs. People got tired of Fido, turned him loose, and he met up with fellow strays, usually taking up residency in empty lots, cemeteries, and deserted areas of the parks where they formed their own outlaw society, mated, and bred generation after generation of wild dogs.

The hair stood up on the back of my neck. My knees shook, and I froze. I flashed my light ahead of me, searching for the beast. The small beam barely penetrated the gloom a few feet in front of me. I cursed silently; why hadn't I brought a large light?

A snarl and more rustling noises. I strained to see, turning slowly, confused. Where were they? How many? God, why hadn't I brought the gun? A growl, then an answer from behind me. I whirled. I felt the air currents stir seconds before a wet, furry body struck me in the shoulder. I dropped the light. I smelled the animal's fetid breath and saw the flash of a crazed eye before I fell.

Teeth ripped at my jacket collar, at my cuffs. I rolled on the ground, grabbed the dog's throat, and flung it aside. Before I had a chance to take a deep breath, a second one was upon me, straddling my body, its fangs snapping at my face. I jerked my head aside and yanked the knife out of its sheath. I swung wildly, an uppercut to the body. The knife thudded into flesh; the thin blade slid off bone, driving deeper into the dog's chest. He yelped once before collapsing on top of me. I heaved the thing aside and struggled to my knees.

Another dog leaped at me. I felt rather than actually saw him as I ducked and slashed. This time I missed. He flung himself onto my back, tore at my clothes. Blood ran down my cheek, and I prayed it belonged to a dog. I stabbed blindly behind my back, felt the blade hit ribs before it slid by them, and the dog dropped off me.

I thought it was over then. I brushed the tears running down my cheeks, gasped for air, scrubbed the blood off my face, and rubbed my aching shoulder muscles.

I don't know what alerted me, but suddenly I realized I wasn't alone. I held my breath and heard panting sounds ahead of me, maybe three, four feet away. I groped for the flashlight on the ground and pointed it in the direction of the panting. He was evil—black with pointed ears, a mixture of Doberman and something. His tongue lolled out as he stared at me. Blood poured from his shoulder, though I didn't remember hitting him.

We stared at each other. I joined him in the animal world as I bared my teeth in a feral snarl and guttural sounds came from my throat. He dropped his head, tucked his tail between his legs, and slunk into the dark. I smiled grimly. Those nature programs on Channel Thirteen were right; the dominant animal wins. Bare your teeth and growl; the weaker will capitulate.

Carefully, I checked myself over, relieved to find that all of the blood belonged to the dogs. That saved me from some painful rabies shots.

I didn't dare leave the dogs to be found by the police. One at a time, I lugged the two carcasses to the beach and threw them into the water, hoping they'd float out with the tide.

Sweat and blood soaked my clothes. I gasped for breath, and pains stabbed my chest. Too much exertion, old girl. I was more used to fighting with my brain. I dropped to the sand in the lee of the gull's slab, but he ignored me. I was exhausted, depressed. I'm not by nature a killer of dogs. I reminded myself that these beasts had forfeited all rights to be considered in the same class as Rover on the back porch. They were flat-out killers.

I leaned back against the slab and gazed out to sea, feeling a kinship with those soldiers who might have sat in the same spot during the War of 1812 when Fort Tilden was first constructed as part of the defense against British ships and local Indians. In 1917, the fort had been named in honor of Samuel T. Tilden, a former governor of New York. Six-inch guns and twelve-inch mortars had been placed in what is now Jacob Riis Park. Then, sometime in 1924, the Army had installed two massive sixteen-inch guns with a range of thirty miles and never fired in anger at any invaders. After the Korean War, Fort Tilden had double-missile silos housing Nike missiles. Now it was a peaceful park and beach.

I recalled the facts from an article I had read when I found our beach walk was going to be here. Ironically, I thought, the article hadn't mentioned wild dogs.

"What're you doing here, Abby, old girl?" I muttered. The sea gull stirred, disturbed by my voice. "What makes you think you can find something the police missed? Maybe there's nothing special about this case and you're wasting your time. A routine mugging that went wrong." I paused, shifting into a more comfortable position.

"If you believe that, old girl, I have a bridge for sale I'd like you to see. Why would he be out here in full uniform? Why here anyway?" Was this another touch of irony—murder a general and drop his body in a bunker on a defunct Army base?

I glanced up at the sky where scudding clouds parted enough to reveal a star here and there. "Follow that star," I muttered, heaving myself to my feet.

I trudged to the bunker, hitting it on the first try. Stakes and ribbons with signs denoting a police investigation surrounded the area. I stepped over them and went inside.

It was scary in there—my shadow on the wall, rustling noises—somebody had mentioned rats. I flashed the light around to where the chalk mark outlined the missing body.

I headed for the other end of the tunnel to look around, my footsteps echoing. I flashed my light into an offshoot tunnel and looked down the barrel of a gun. I sucked in my breath and raised the light to find Detective Standish grinning at me as she aimed a powerful flashlight into my eyes.

"Well, well," she said, "Ms. Doyle, I presume. I knew somebody would come back for this."

I couldn't see what she was holding, a glint of silver or something, maybe a medal.

"Could you point your gun and light somewhere else," I said wearily.

She angled the light down and I focused on her hand. She held the general's name tag.

She laughed. "Here we are, woman-to-woman, so to speak."

"I think it used to be man-to-man."

"Times are changing, Doyle."

I shrugged. "How long have you been sitting here?"

"Quite a while. I'm a patient woman, Doyle. Funny, I didn't think it would be you."

"Well, then, can I put my hands down? Bursitis, you know."

She laughed. "Lean against the wall and spread 'em."

She gingerly patted my wet clothes. "No gun. Oh, oh, what's this?" she said as she discovered my knife. "The old knife-in-the-boot trick." She shined her light on it. "Blood! Careless, Doyle, very careless." She examined me closer. "You're a mess."

"That blood is from a couple of wild dogs. Didn't you hear me out there fighting for my life?"

"Oh, yes. That. I was rooting for the dogs."

Dropping my hands, I turned to face her. She stepped back. Her gun pointed at my stomach.

"Look, Standish, both of us are too old to play these childish games. I don't go around murdering generals, and I think you know that. I think you also know that I sometimes stick my nose into police business, especially when it means big bucks for me. I have an idea you resent that, so you're doing this little tap dance on me."

She smiled as she stuck her gun back into its holster and passed me a thermos. "Have a cup of coffee. As a matter of fact, I did run a check on you this afternoon. Interesting."

I shrugged. She continued.

"Divorced, one daughter, a freshman in college. Respected businesswoman. In fact, considered among the top ten in your field. You have a pistol permit, also, a six-figure income on which you seem to pay your fair share of taxes."

I raised my eyebrows. "You have an in with Internal Revenue?"

"Not exactly. Anyway, you take on selected cases for hefty fees or barter as in the case of your fancy apartment. By the way, I'd like to see it sometime. Sounds interesting."

"Any time—with a search warrant. And to set the record straight, the apartment was a gift from the factory owner."

She ignored that. "You make good money from being a legitimate efficiency expert. The mayor could use you to streamline the police department. You're interested in Save Anything organizations from whales to cockroaches."

"No cockroaches yet. Seriously, Standish, what are you leading up to?"

"I think you or somebody in your happy little group is involved in General Thorne's death. Is that clear enough?"

I studied her face. She was serious. It hadn't taken her long to identify Thorne. What did she know that I didn't? Maybe she only knew his name from the tag.

"Standish, I'll make you an offer. You give me your big flashlight and go outside for ten minutes. Then I'll tell you everything I know."

She shook her head, a grin slowly turning up the corners of her mouth. "Doyle, you're the damndest person I've ever met. You want me to leave you here to plant something, using my flashlight to boot?"

"Trust me."

"Said the spider to the fly." She chewed her lip. "Maybe I'm more of an idiot than I thought, but here." She traded flashlights with me and left.

I searched the area where the body had been found. There was nothing of interest. I considered dropping the lighter in a dark corner, but I didn't think that would really fool Standish. Honesty is the best policy, I told myself.

"Okay, you can come in now."

Standish looked around suspiciously. "Well, where's the planted evidence proving you and your jolly gang of do-gooders couldn't possibly be involved? Also, tell me everything you know."

I told her everything I knew, omitting only the construction project. "I forgot to give you this today," I said, handing her the lighter.

She glared at me. "I could book you for withholding evidence. Where'd you find it?"

"In his pocket. I was looking for a match to light a candle. I'm really sorry. I dropped it into my pocket and forgot about it until I got home."

"Doyle, for some stupid reason, I believe you. Which pocket did you find it in?"

Closing my eyes, I visualized myself patting the victim's pockets. "Strange. Left rear pocket. Not exactly where everyone carries a lighter, is it?"

"Obviously not his lighter," she said as she noticed the initial J. "You have a Jill in your group, don't you?"

I laughed. "Mother of six. Really, Standish, you'll have to do better than that."

She nodded, grinning in spite of herself. "Do you have a client for this one?"

"Nope. Just idle curiosity and self-defense if you persist in considering us suspects. By the way, where did you get his name tag?"

Standish stared at me. Then she shrugged. "Why don't you run along and let me get on with waiting for somebody else to turn up—maybe the J who belongs to this lighter."

I paused at the door. "One more thing. How did the general get here? Drive? Walk? Parachute?"

"The dry uniform bothers you too?" She rubbed her chin. "I don't know. If you find out before I do, let me know."

"Right, Standish. Good night and good hunting. Watch out for those dogs."

She called after me, "The tag was in the bushes beside the road."

From the beach I looked back toward the bunker— a dark mound. I imagined Standish sitting in the dark, waiting. I didn't think anyone else would show up.

The trip back to my car seemed shorter. I've noticed that return trips always seem shorter. I wonder why.

FOUR

Midnight

I SHOWERED THE STINK of the dogs off me, made myself some coffee, and stretched out on the couch in my office. Standish's review of my life had reminded me of my daughter Jackie. She had elected not to spend the holidays with me, and she was beyond the age where a judge's edict could force her to do anything.

Jackie had chosen to live with her father before fathers were fashionable. I always suspected California had more to do with her choice than undying love for her father. She was a typical California girl—fair like her father, bronze tan, surfer's muscles, a white toothpaste-ad smile. Fortunately, she had my brains. She was a freshman at Stanford.

Sometimes I wondered what it would have been like to have her underfoot all the time. Would we have gotten along? She's self-sufficient and stubborn like me. She always projects such an aura of coolness. Sometimes I think she's not too crazy about either of her parents.

I paid most of her expenses because, as the judge said, I made much more money than her father. Brandon, a minor-league actor, was perpetually unemployed. In the sixties, he'd been a feature actor in several beachboy movies, but there weren't many roles for aging beachboys these days.

"Time for bed, old girl." I stood up, then noticed the red light on my answer phone. Sighing, I punched the button.

"Mother, call me when you get in. Jackie."

I sighed again. I just wanted to go to bed. I always suspect that people who call their mothers "Mother" do so out of a wary respect. Those who really love their mothers call them "Mom" or some other endearing name.

I slipped her card into the automatic dialer. Click, click, ring. "Hello."

"Jackie, this is your mother." Two could play this game. "You called."

"Yes. I wanted to wish you a Happy New Year."

"You could have done it in person," I said mildly with a minimum of recrimination in my tone. Ordinarily, I don't believe in laying guilt trips on anybody, but Standish and the dogs had put me in a sour mood.

"Is something wrong? You sound strange."

Ah, the beach girl has a perceptive nature. "I'm up to my ears in a murder case. You might even say I'm one of the suspects and I'm not used to being a suspect. Other than that, everything is grand in this New Year. Do you need money?"

She laughed. "You? A suspect? But you're always on the side of the angels."

"This time the angels may well be the Corps of Engineers. As you know, I'm not usually on their side.

One of their generals was murdered this morning—I should say yesterday morning. And some of my little pals and I were in the area and stumbled upon the body."

"Your annual New Year's Day walk, right?"

"Right."

"Wow! That's really exciting." Did I detect a note of interest in my daughter's voice? "Hey, I don't have to be back to school for two weeks. I'll come and help you."

Amazing. My daughter, for the first time in years, actually wanted to spend some time with her poor, old mother.

"I don't know, Jackie. I'm going to be pretty busy on this. I could even be in jail." That's laying it on pretty thick, Doyle. "But, if you really want to, come ahead."

"Great, I'll catch a plane and be there early in the morning. Don't worry about picking me up, I'll take a cab. Bye." Click. She was gone before I could say anything.

This was certainly a strange way to start a new year—murder, Jackie coming to stay willingly. I decided to sleep on it.

FIVE

Saturday Morning

THE BELL RANG, and I pushed the general away. The bell rang again. Opening my eyes, I realized it was my doorbell and glared at the clock. Seven.

I shambled out to the hall and flicked on the scanner. Jackie shivering in a light suede jacket, stared plaintively up at the camera. I pressed the elevator button.

Bursting out of the elevator car a few minutes later, she gave me a quick hug and said, "Hi, Mother, what's for breakfast? I'm starved," as she brushed by me.

I followed her inside. She was gazing at the skyline.

I examined her and noted a few changes. The California beach girl was maturing. Her blond hair was cut short now, like mine. She seemed taller, stood straighter, and her bearing was more purposeful. Maybe she wasn't going to slouch and charm her way through life like her father after all.

She turned, smiled. "What are you staring at?"

"You. You're different. It's been over a year since I saw you last. Changes occur rapidly at your age."

"Breakfast?"

"Coming up."

She perched on a stool at the kitchen counter, watching me fry Canadian bacon and scramble eggs. "Tell me all about the case," she said.

I filled her in on the details.

"Standish thinks our mild-mannered environmentalists might be bloodthirsty killers. I guess we should be flattered. Sort of belies the image of doddering old folks in tennis shoes."

I served her breakfast, then nibbled on a piece of bacon and toast myself.

"What brings you to New York? You usually spend vacations with your father."

She shrugged. "Things just sounded more exciting here." She brushed her hair back. "I didn't realize we look a little alike. Must be my new haircut."

I smiled. "We still won't pass for twins. You must be tired. Why don't you take a nap. I have a few things to do this morning."

"About the case?"

"No. About groceries and errands. Now, get."

JACKIE'S PRESENCE might be a problem. I found myself thinking about her instead of the case as I ambled through an empty supermarket. But then, why should I think about the general? Standish probably had the case solved by now. And nobody had offered me anything to solve it.

I returned to a silent apartment, where I glanced at Jackie's door, which was closed. After I put away the groceries, I puttered around the kitchen for a few minutes before going reluctantly into my office.

The first message on the phone recorder began, "Doyle, pay attention."

I did.

"I'm sending you a package containing ten thousand dollars. Forget the Thorne case."

I replayed the message. Short and sweet—ten thousand dollars' worth of sugar. For nothing. I had been considering just letting Standish solve the case, but now my interest was piqued. Who? Why? Somebody with a pipeline into the police station? Why the whispering? Could it be somebody I knew?

The second message was from Ricky. "About the LaChance company, it's one of the best corporate concealment jobs I've ever seen. LaChance has a large office complex in the World Trade Center. It appears to be a private company. Two men, Jacob Reese and James Radway, seem to be the chief executives. Their operating officers are up-front and so is the board of directors. However, the real ownership—probably a holding company—is something else. I'll continue checking on Monday when everything opens up again. Happy New Year."

Two J's, I thought, too pat. Besides, men were supposed to use their last initials. I had a hunch the cigarette lighter had nothing to do with either of them.

I was always amazed at how difficult it was to discover the real owners of some large American corporations. Maybe it wasn't even important to know.

The third message stated a telephone number on Long Island an a request to call as soon as possible, in a woman's voice. I checked the rest of my messages before dialing the mystery number.

A man answered. "Thorne residence, may I help you?"

"This is Abigail Doyle. Someone at this number asked me to call."

"One moment, please. Mrs. Thorne wishes to speak with you."

Mrs. Thorne! The general's wife? I felt like Alice in Wonderland. That was the last name I had expected to hear.

An elderly woman with a bar of steel in her voice icily asked, "Are you *the* Abigail Doyle, the efficiency expert who worked once for Mrs. Conrad Smythe-Lewis of Philadelphia?"

I recalled the case—a very wealthy woman with a junkie son who had eloped with a family diamond worth a million dollars.

"Yes, I'm that Doyle. And who are you?"

"I am Vivian Thorne, General Martin Thorne's mother. My son has been murdered, and I'm not satisfied with the police investigation. I would like you to take charge."

I thought of poor Standish's face if she could hear Mrs. Thorne telling me to take charge. "Mrs. Thorne, are you aware that I'm a possible suspect in that case?"

Silence. Then, the first crack in the steel. "I—I don't understand. Mrs. Smythe-Lewis recommended you highly."

"And well she should. However, by a quirk of fate, I was with the group that found your son's body. Also, that group is antagonistic toward the Corps of Engineers. Do you still want to hire me?"

"Did you have anything to do with his death?"

"No, ma'am."

"Could you come and see me?"

"Yes. Where do you live?"

After she gave me directions to her Oyster Bay estate, I said, "I'll be there as soon as possible."

I called my favorite limousine service and ordered something elegant, but subdued, for a visit to old money.

Jackie padded up behind me. "Limousine?"

I jumped.

"You forgot I was here, didn't you?"

I laughed. "Sort of. At least during that conversation. Want to go with me? You'll have to wait outside."

"Sure. Sounds like fun, riding around in a limo."

"Coffee's in the kitchen. I have to change."

I SELECTED a classic beige wool blazer and matching wool slacks. I wanted to look prosperous but understated. The clothes and the limo were all calculated to inspire confidence in Mrs. Thorne.

"Mother, the car's here," Jackie called.

I'd been so deep in thought, I hadn't heard the bell.

Jackie stared at me when I entered the kitchen. "Wow! I thought detectives were supposed to have a seedy look."

"I'm not a detective. I'm an efficiency expert and well respected in my field. And don't you forget it, young lady." I smiled. "I'll bet you tell your friends that your mother is a cross between Sam Spade and Miss Marple, smoking a big cigar and dithering around the village green solving crimes."

She had the grace to blush. "I don't really talk about you much."

"Black-sheep mother." I shrugged. "It's okay, kid. When I was your age, I didn't mention that my mother was a sumo wrestler either."

"Oh, Mother! Can't you be serious?"

I tapped an imaginary cigar the way Groucho used to do and growled, "Shortly, I'll be very serious. Let's go. Michaels charges by the hour."

IT'S ALWAYS COMFORTING to sweep along the Long Island Expressway, wrapped in the deep blue womb of a Michaels limousine. Through the tinted window, I watched the people passing by. Some stared, wondering who was inside the limo. Rock star? Movie queen? Politician? Gangster? Others flashed disdainful looks. Still others rigidly ignored us. Jackie seemed fascinated by the television set. I hoped her father hadn't raised a vidiot.

Oyster Bay ranges from the tacky to the grand. Sand pits, shopping centers, luxurious mansions. We swept through the town and around the harbor into the domain of the rich. A small plaque set in a stone gate discreetly announced Thorne. We drove at least a quarter of a mile along a tree-lined driveway. As we rounded a bend, we saw the elegant brick Georgian mansion on a hill overlooking the bay.

The car glided to a stop, and I waited for the chauffeur to open my door. Jackie was staring at the house. "Nice place," she said in an awed voice, "like a movie set."

I winked. "See you later. Don't wander off."

I eyed the butler who opened the door. He was tall, dignified, and English. He looked beyond me at the limo and dismissed it as rented. His nose and eyebrows plainly labeled me as a peasant.

I smiled. "Mrs. Thorne is expecting me. Abigail Doyle."

"Follow me, please. Madame is in the solarium."

He escorted me through a spacious center hall. Old portraits of military men in full-dress uniforms stared down at me. Everything was old—old wood, old silver, old paintings. The woman waiting for me was also old, old money and impeccable taste. She studied me as I crossed the room.

Waving a dismissal, she said, "That will be all, Jared. Ms. Doyle—you see, I'm a modern woman."

I smiled, half bowed. I wanted to curtsy. This must be what it felt like to meet Queen Elizabeth for the first time. Mrs. Thorne was slight and short but ramrod straight. She wore a simple black silk dress set off by a single strand of pearls. Her expression was composed, her eyes alert.

Mentally, I shook myself. Wake up, Doyle, this is America where everyone is equal, but this lady is more equal than anyone I've ever met. I wanted to escape; I didn't want to discuss her dead son. A murdered son in this house was a sacrilege. All related to this woman should only die in their beds, counting their money. How could a son of hers be so venal or so desperate to sell out to a large corporation? Something was askew about this whole case.

"Is something wrong, Ms. Doyle?" she asked.

"No. I'm sorry. The room and the view are so beautiful, I'm afraid I just drifted off for a moment."

"Strange, I always thought efficiency experts were very self-possessed. After all, it must take a great deal of confidence to tell someone how to run a business. Or are you really more of a detective?" The tone of her voice equated detective with prostitute.

"Both are honorable professions, Mrs. Thorne. Now, about your son. What can I do for you?"

For the first time I discerned a crack in her facade. She melted a little; her eyes glistened as she fidgeted with a bronze horse on the table next to her and looked beyond me out the window.

Softly, she said, "My late husband was a general too. West Point. In spite of all the Thorne money, the men served their country in every war since the Revolution. Martin was the only one of our children to follow the military tradition. He is—was—my youngest son. The other two went into business and law. I was very proud of Martin. I want you to find his murderer.''

I nodded. "This may seem like an impertinent question, but did your son need money?''

The silence grew palpable. I waited. Very important to be patient in this business, to outlast a silence. How much money was enough money? I wondered. Did the Thorne companies have anything to do with building condominiums?

"Martin never discussed his affairs with me. Of course, he had his salary and all the perquisites that go with being a general. He had a trust fund from his grandfather's estate, and would have received another one upon my death." Her voice faltered. She collected herself.

"His wife also has a trust fund. She's one of the Philadelphia Carpenters. As far as I know, they didn't live beyond their means. I don't think Martin gambled or kept a mistress or anything like that." In a low tone more to herself than to me, she added, "But who really knows her children?''

She stared out the window. Except for the slight quiver in her lips, one would think that she was unfeeling about her son's death. But then the rich are taught to conceal their feelings. The old English stiff-upper-lip syndrome.

"Mrs. Thorne, the police will do their best to find the murderer of your son and probably will, eventually. To hire me will be very expensive. Your friend, Mrs. Smythe-Lewis, must have told you that I'm a luxury." I smiled. "And if I take the case, I will expect full cooperation from you and everybody associated with you."

"You're not exactly here hat in hand, are you?"

"No, ma'am."

She moved around the room, picking up a statue here, straightening a picture there. I noticed she had a slight limp.

Finally, she turned to look at me. "I will hire you."

I stood up. "Fine. Give me a check for one thousand dollars as a retainer. That will enable me to prove to the police, if necessary, that I have a client and am entitled to remain silent on certain questions."

"That's very clever, isn't it? If you're the murderer, you're using me to hide behind." Her eyes challenged me.

"Mrs. Thorne, if I had killed your son, I wouldn't come near you." I smiled. "The check protects both of us. It means anything you tell me is privileged information."

"Follow me, please."

She led me through the house to an imposing library with floor-to-ceiling bookcases covering two walls. I itched to get my hands on the books as I scanned the titles, looking for clues about the people who lived or had lived in this house. The selection was eclectic—mysteries, children's stories, military histories, well-worn leatherbound classics, art books, engineering texts. Suddenly I was aware of Mrs. Thorne standing behind me.

"Do you like books?" she asked.

"Unfortunately, yes. I'd rather read than anything."

"Odd, I would think you were more a person of action," she said, handing me a check.

"Thank you. One more thing—would you arrange for me to see your son's widow right away. If you have any influence with her, tell her to answer all of my questions."

"I have no influence with Lydia," she said wryly. "I don't think anyone has. I'm afraid, Ms. Doyle, you're going to earn this retainer just talking to her."

I looked at her thoughtfully. "Why do you say that? Do you have a problem with your daughter-in-law? What kind of woman is she?"

"I prefer not to answer."

"May I remind you that without your cooperation, I'm not interested in taking this case. I can't work with one hand tied behind my back." I extended the check to her.

She waved it away. Her tone was icy. "I hope there's a line between legitimate investigation and prying."

"There is." I smiled. "Tell me about Lydia."

"She's the mother of my favorite grandchild, Roxanne," she said. Staring at a point over my head, she added in a lifeless voice, "Lydia is very much her own person. She never became a Thorne, never had any concern for the Thorne traditions. I never knew what Martin saw in her. Of course, her family background is impeccable. She's a cultured, intelligent woman, everything I should desire in a daughter-in-law, but we've never been close. I hardly see her."

"How did your son feel about her?"

She shrugged. "Apparently he loved her. I don't really know. Martin and I did not discuss his marriage."

"How often did you see Martin?"

She winced at my use of his first name. "As often as necessary and appropriate to people in our state."

Whatever that meant. I folded the check and put it in my pocket. I paused at the door to look back at Mrs. Thorne, who was standing at the window, her back rigid. I wondered for a moment if she was crying, but dismissed that as unlikely.

Jackie and the chauffeur were leaning against the car, gazing at the bay. Jackie noticed me. "Hey, how'd it go?"

I shrugged. "She hired me."

I repeated Mrs. Thorne's directions to her son's farm to the chauffeur. Twenty minutes later we entered a tree-lined country lane with a simple wooden sign hanging on the white gate that read *The Farm*.

I pointed at the sign. "The general must have had an Eisenhower complex."

We drove up the lane until a white mansion came into view. I asked the chauffeur to stop for a mo-

ment. It looked as if Tara had been transplanted from
the set of *Gone With the Wind*. The fields were bor-
dered by white rail fences. A large barn and stables
were also white. We parked near the barn, where we
got out and waited as a woman on a large white horse
rode toward us. I figured this was Lydia Thorne, and
I wondered what her game was going to be.

Before I could say anything, she said, "Mrs. Thorne
called. I always take my ride this time of day." She
surveyed me coolly. "Do you ride?"

I smiled. "If it's necessary."

"Very good. I have a horse ready for you." She
turned toward the stables.

I looked heavenward and exhaled noisily. Without
looking back at Jackie, I muttered, "I bet you thought
this business was all fun. You didn't realize how dangerous it could be. She's probably putting me on a
special killer horse with a burr under his saddle." I
winked, giving her a Bogart sneer. "See you later,
kid."

I hitched up my imaginary chaps and strode to the
stable, wishing I had succumbed to the New York fad
of wearing cowboy boots everywhere. My Wallabys
would have to do.

Lydia Thorne waited, tall and erect in the saddle.
She was at least six feet tall. Her long salt-and-pepper
hair was tied back in a ponytail. She wore proper riding clothes—polished boots, fawn-colored jodhpurs,
and a cocoa-colored soft leather jacket. Tension lines
tugged at the corners of her lips, and her blue eyes had

all the warmth of a glacier. Her hands were large, easy on the reins. Half of her left thumb was missing.

A groom was holding my horse, a black stallion with one ear forward and one back, an attitude of "try to get aboard, sister, and I'll annihilate you." Stepping forward, I pulled his front ear down and whispered, "You big bastard, you try anything funny with me and I'll ride you down the middle of the LIE." The horse snorted. I stepped back. "Nice horse," I said. The groom gave me a leg up. "It's your parade, Mrs. Thorne, lead on."

She glared at me. Whatever her expectations were, they didn't materialize, because this horse knew I was at least his equal. During part of my misspent youth, I had helped my uncle break quarter horses. Always show them you're the boss had been his credo.

She cantered out of the yard, and I followed. Since it is a little difficult to carry on a conversation with a horse's rump, I urged my black beauty to speed up. When I pulled even with her, she looked at me, an evil grin spreading across her face.

"Let's race," she yelled, spurring her horse, who leaped ahead.

That's all the black needed. The white disappearing into the trees was like a goad to him. Before I could settle firmly into the saddle, he sprinted, almost leaving me in midair, but I managed to keep my balance.

I prayed my horse knew where the path was. From where I was sitting, it looked like a solid wall of pine trees ahead. Unerringly, he hit a narrow opening. Entering the woods was like going from light to dark. My eyes slowly adjusted. Around a bend ahead I glimpsed a flash of white. We were gaining. Suddenly we erupted into a sunlit clearing. I reined in the black, and he stood, head down, sides heaving.

Puzzled, I dismounted and leaned against his sweating side while I scanned the clearing. No white horse. No Lydia. I listened. Silence. I shivered as the cold air congealed my perspiration.

"What kind of game is she playing?" I asked the horse.

The clearing was the size of a couple of circus rings put together. I tied the horse to a branch while I walked around the circle, looking for another exit. I found a barely discernible path on the far right side and pushed through the sparse branches. Fifty yards away, the path curved left, disappearing from view again.

Why take me out in the woods and lose me? I wondered. I'll be back, I promised. Lydia Thorne needed some checking.

I headed slowly back toward the stables. From the meadow, I saw Jackie and the groom pacing back and forth, and waved. They waved back and trotted toward me, so I urged the black into a gallop.

"What's wrong?" I asked as I reined the horse to a stop.

"Are you all right?" Jackie asked anxiously.

"Certainly. Just a nice country ride. Except my riding companion disappeared into thin air." I frowned at the groom. "Would you know anything about that?"

He was a man in his sixties with a seamed, leathery outdoor face and mildly depressed gray eyes. A man, I thought, who needed his job and hated his boss.

Hitching up his pants, he spat tobacco juice, then wiped his mouth. "If I tell you, will you keep it to yourself?" I nodded. He studied me, deciding that my simple nod was as valid as a profuse verbal assurance. "There's a cabin back there where she goes. You reached the clearing?" I nodded. "Well, there's a hidden path off it that leads to the cabin."

I looked over my shoulder. "Can she see us from the cabin?"

He spat again. "Yuh. There's a rise near the cabin that gives you a partial view of the stables and the lane, but not the house. She didn't want to talk to you. That's why she gave you Midnight's Satan. He's a hard horse to handle, but he surely took to you."

I smiled. "In other words, he was supposed to break my neck, or at the very least, leave me tongue-tied with fear. Nice horse." I patted his neck. He snorted in agreement.

The groom scratched his head. "What did you whisper in Satan's ear?" When I repeated my threat, he chuckled. "I'll have to remember that."

I slid off the horse and handed the reins to the groom. As we started toward the stables I asked, "Did you know the general well?"

"Nope. He hated horses. Didn't spend much time here. Stayed in Washington. He came here for holidays because of the daughter. That was about it." He spat. "Oh, he also showed up when she had some fancy charity do or something like that."

"In other words they weren't a close, loving couple."

He spat. "You said it, I didn't."

Jackie, who had been listening attentively, asked, "What'll you do now?"

I winked. "Mrs. Lydia Thorne has told me more than I would have found out from my innocuous for-the-widow questions." I rubbed Satan's nose and handed the groom a twenty along with the reins. "Tell Mrs. Thorne thanks for the ride. Tell her I'm sorry I lost her and couldn't wait for her return."

Jackie looked at me curiously as we headed for the limo. "Why wouldn't she talk to you?"

I shrugged. "Maybe she has something to hide. Maybe she's grief-stricken. Then again, she might just want to annoy her mother-in-law." I scanned the fields for a sign of the white horse. I smiled. "Maybe she just didn't like my looks. Let's go home."

SIX

Saturday Afternoon

I PUSHED THE BUTTON on my answering machine. No
messages. I hated it when a case just stopped. I had no
ideas. The most intriguing part of the whole day had
been the widow's reaction. What was she hiding, or
was this just the normal dislike of the rich for personal questions?

I would even have welcomed Standish's presence,
though I didn't have much hope for our future relationship. She resented me. Cops regard crime as their
private fiefdom.

Crime doesn't stop on weekends, but business does.
I suspected the answer to the general's death was to be
found in financial records.

I punched all the facts into my interior computer,
but no inspired answers shot out. I have an unusual
ability—practically everything I read or hear or see
becomes a permanent part of my memory, recalled by
going into a trance while my brain shuffles through its
collection of facts.

Jackie knocked at my office door. "Got a minute?"

She was wearing an expression that indicated serious mother-daughter talk.

My God, she's pregnant, I thought wildly. Drugs. Expelled from school. Dying from some disease. All the pleasant things that go through a parent's mind.

Poker-faced, I waved at the chair across from my desk. "Sit down. What's your problem?"

"Mother, could I live with you?"

I stared at her. "I think I need a drink," I muttered. When I returned from the bar with a glass of Chablis for me and a Coke for Jackie, I asked, "What exactly do you mean by live with me?"

"I'd like to transfer to St. John's next fall and study law. Eventually, I want to specialize in maritime law. I'd like to live here."

"What does your father say?"

"I haven't told him yet. I wanted to clear it with you first."

"Don't you realize what this will do to him?"

She shook her head.

I smiled fiendishly. "It means he'll have to work for a living. I will no longer have to pay that exorbitant monthly fee to him."

She stared at her feet. "He has a live-in girlfriend, Rita. She's twenty." She looked at me. "What monthly fee?"

"Didn't you know? All these years, I've been paying for you and indirectly supporting him in the style in which I wanted you to live? Did you really think he bought your clothes, paid for your education, your vacations, your orthodontist, your car? Did you really think he made enough money from those beach-boy roles to pay for all that?"

"I—I just didn't think about it." Tears formed in her eyes. "When he told me you didn't want me, I just didn't think about you much."

I flashed back nine years to a California courtroom scene, forever engraved in my heart. A black-robed woman judge with accusatory eyes was informing me that she had just awarded custody of my daughter to her father because that was who she wanted to live with, and since I made more money, I could pay child support, which would escalate as my income grew until Jackie was eighteen or finished college or moved out of her father's home. I had been shocked—devastated that Jackie had selected her father. So shocked, I hadn't asked any questions.

"What do you mean, I didn't want you?"

Jackie fiddled with her glass, unable to look me in the eye. "He—he told me you were moving to New York, where you had an important job. He said I'd be a drag on your career. He said you wouldn't tell me that because you were too kind, but that you really didn't want me."

I interrupted. "I can't believe that a ten-year-old daughter of mine could have believed that hogwash. Why didn't you ask me?"

"He told me not to mention it because it would upset you too much."

"You bet it would have upset somebody. Him! He would have had to work all these years."

I sipped my wine until I regained my composure. "You'll never know how hurt I was that day, how hurt I have been all these years until I just more or less put you out of my mind. Days would go by and I would forget I had a daughter. Then I'd read about a newborn tiger cub at the Bronx Zoo and think, Jackie would love to see it, and then realize you weren't here. We could have shared so many things. Now I don't really know you, and obviously you don't know me."

"I used to tell people you were dead," she said quietly. "I resented you so much. I felt so unwanted."

"What's done is done," I said philosophically. I didn't know how to react. I wasn't sure I was ready to be a full-time mother with a teenager underfoot all the time. My life and work were structured. Part of me said welcome the change wholeheartedly, part of me said go slow.

Jackie looked at me expectantly. "Well, what do you think?"

"Jackie, I don't want you to take this wrong, but maybe you should continue at Stanford and spend your summers and holidays here." Her eyes filled with tears. "No, stop. Hear me out. I lead a very demanding life, juggling two careers. This is not only my home, it's my office. Sometimes my life is dangerous. Consequently, you would be in danger, too. Also, New York is not California. Your life-style would change drastically. Subways and buses instead of that fancy sports car."

"I can handle it. I'm not Daddy's little girl anymore or should I say Daddy's little meal ticket," she added wickedly.

"Whoa. Let's take it one step at a time. First, you can move out of your father's house. This will officially be your home. You'll spend your holidays and summer vacations here. Then we'll discuss the college transfer this summer. You might want to finish your undergraduate work at Stanford and do your graduate work at an eastern college. Now, run along." I chuckled as I reached for the phone. "Ah, I must call your father."

SEVEN

Saturday Evening

JACKIE AND I spent the rest of the day making arrangements for the shipment of her belongings and hashing out the ground rules for her demotion from guest to daughter. I made a pizza for dinner. We had just finished eating when the obvious doorbell rang.

I checked the scanner. A grim-faced Standish was staring at the camera. I gave her instructions for the elevator. While I waited, I wondered what she wanted. She certainly doesn't look happy, I thought. This was no social call.

When the elevator door slid open, I said, "Detective Standish, I presume. Do you have a warrant?"

She brandished a piece of paper. "As a matter of fact, no. But you'd better listen to what I've just heard from the Nassau County police. They might arrive here shortly."

Lydia Thorne leaped to mind. She'd filed some kind of complaint against me. "I can explain that," I said.

Surprised, Standish peered at me. "How'd you know she was dead?"

"Wait a minute. Are we talking about the same thing?" Jackie wandered into the room. Distracted, I said, "Detective Standish, my daughter Jackie. Jackie, would you excuse us, please." She gave me an annoyed look as she left the room. "Now, what's this all about?"

Standish meandered around the room, pausing to ponder a Miró print or a Lizzul seascape. She stopped at the window framing Manhattan and rocked back and forth on her heels, her hands clasped behind her back as she gazed at the skyline.

Impatiently, I chewed my lip, but I was determined not to break the silence. After all, I was an expert at using the old silence ploy. But who was dead? Lydia? The general's mother? Someone else? Nassau County police meant it had to be one of the Thornes. A regular epidemic in that family.

Finally, Standish turned around. I noticed the fatigue lines around her eyes and lips. She looked as if she hadn't been to bed for two days, and her clothes were rumpled. For some reason I felt sorry for her.

"Have you eaten?" I asked. She shook her head. "Sit down. A couple more minutes won't make any difference."

"Thanks," she said when I placed a ham sandwich and coffee on the table beside her. "Nice place." She took a bite out of her sandwich. "I didn't realize how hungry I was." Her smile twisted. "You're not making this easy."

"Standish, you came alone. So whatever is going on, you're going to give me a fair shake. If you thought I was some kind of homicidal maniac, you sure as hell would be crazy to be sitting there, calmly eating that poisoned sandwich.''

She grimaced. ''I think you're either crazy or some kind of sly fox. Lydia Thorne is dead.''

I groaned. ''Let me guess. She was found in her cabin with a knife in her back, while her faithful white horse grazed outside. The groom said the only visitor was one private detective, Abby Doyle. Am I right, so far?''

She nodded. ''On the money. You had access. You disappeared into the woods with her. You returned alone pretty winded. You had wanted to talk to her, but when you returned, you told the groom you'd lost her in the woods. You were quite nonchalant about the whole thing.''

I shrugged. ''I lost her in the woods. So what? When will the Nassau police be here?''

''They'll probably get lost. This place is difficult to find.''

I smiled. ''I like it that way.'' I glanced at the detective, who seemed lost in thought. ''I was sure the general's death had something to do with his military duties, but now I'm not so sure. She wouldn't have anything to do with them. A personal matter, you think?''

Standish stood up and glared at me. ''I have one question to ask. Did you murder Mrs. Thorne?''

''No.'' I stared at the red and green lights on top of the Empire State Building while I tried to remember something. "I think Mrs. Thorne might have been trying to do a little bodily harm to me."

"What do you mean?"

I related my experience with Satan, emphasizing that a poor or mediocre rider would have been injured or killed by the beast.

"Standish, are we friends or antagonists?"

She shrugged. "I haven't made up my mind about that, Doyle. As a police officer, I feel I should haul your tail down to headquarters. As a person, I sort of feel you're on the level." She waved a hand to indicate the room. "As an underpaid civil servant, I should resent all this. Too bad we don't have a per crime rate."

"Hate to disillusion you, Standish, but most of this was bought by money made the old-fashioned way— I earned it. I stood around in drafty, antiquated factories and found out how to make them more productive. I sat in overheated offices, watching the paper flow, and told them how to route it more efficiently.

"Granted, I have a gift. Probably because I'm basically lazy, I can see how to do things easier, faster, cheaper. I also apply that gift to criminal cases occasionally. I'm not your competitor, and I hope I'm not a suspect. Standish, I couldn't do what you do every day. To me, a murder case is like a crossword puzzle, recreation."

She winced. "Doyle, that's even worse. Recreation, for God's sake! Those are real dead people out there."

The doorbell silenced her. The screen showed a beefy sergeant in uniform and a thin man in a gray three-piece suit.

Standish looked at the screen. "I don't want to be found here."

"Neither do I. That looks suspiciously like a warrant in the sergeant's hand."

She glanced at me. "How're you planning to escape?"

I grinned. "Why, with you, of course."

"Are you crazy?" she sputtered. "I could be liable for obstructing justice."

"I haven't got all night to argue. Do you really think justice will be served by my spending the night in a Nassau county jail? Come on." I grabbed a jacket and stopped in Jackie's room. After a brief explanation, I said, "Let them in. You don't know where I am. If they have a search warrant, let them search. If they don't and try anyway, call Maria Palmieri, my attorney. I'll call you later."

I dragged Standish into my bedroom, where I pushed a concealed button in a narrow floor-to-ceiling bookcase. The bookcase swung back, revealing a narrow stairway.

"This takes us into the factory. From there we can get out through a fire door on the far side of the building."

"Do you think you should be showing me your secrets?"

"Standish, I think you're an honorable person."

"And I think you're a nut," she muttered. "Ouch! Damn!"

"Forgot to tell you to duck. You all right?"

"Yeh. This place's for midgets. Let's get out of here. It's spooky."

"Great place to hide a body," I said in a sinister Peter Lorre voice.

We threaded our way between covered machines. A dog growled. Standish stiffened beside me. "What's that?"

"Only Apollo." I whistled. "Here, boy." A Doberman sidled around a table, his white teeth gleaming in the glow from my flashlight. "Hey, boy," I crooned as I rubbed his head. "He's harmless, if you know him. That whistle tells him I'm a friend."

"After last night, I thought you'd be off dogs," she needled me.

I opened the fire door. The wind was cold. I shivered.

"All quiet. Where's your car?"

"Across the street from the front of your place."

"Let's hope they've left no one outside."

We trotted up the street, keeping in the lee of the building. The police car, parked across the mouth of the alley, blocked my car.

"Let's go," I said. We sprinted across the street to Standish's car.

Standish started the motor. "Now where?"

"There's a gas station on Northern Boulevard beyond Shea Stadium. The owner sometimes rents me a car. Drop me there."

Her teeth flashed in that shark grin of hers. "No way. Where you go, I go."

"Let's not get biblical about it. I don't think you really want to go with me."

"Either I go or we go back upstairs."

I sighed. "Standish, I want to visit that cabin in the woods."

"You're crazy," she blurted. "It's probably crawling with cops."

"I doubt it. They should be through by now. I didn't see it this afternoon and I want to see it now. Lydia Thorne spent a lot of time there. Maybe she left some answers behind. Now, will you just drop me off."

"I'm going with you."

"You could get in trouble."

"Only if I'm caught. I'm depending upon you to make sure that doesn't happen. How do I get to this place?"

After I gave her directions, we drove in silence for several miles while I brooded.

We were almost there when she said, "I don't like the country. I don't like it when there's nothing but trees for miles. I don't like the silence. I don't like the dark."

I blinked out of my trance. "You don't like the country! You're going to see a lot of it before this night is over."

I recognized the lane leading to the Thorne farm. A quarter of a mile down the road, I said, "Pull over. The cabin should be straight back from here."

A horrified expression crossed her face. "I thought we could drive to it," she yelped.

"No way, pal. I don't want the groom to spot us and call the cops. We have to walk." In a spooky whisper, I added, "Through yon darkling woods where there are bats, reptiles, and creatures that go bump in the night." I swear she actually shuddered. I laughed. "Or you can wait in the car."

"How far?"

"At least a mile, maybe more. I might have a little trouble hitting it on the first try in the dark. I haven't been there, but I have a pretty good idea where it is if I can find that clearing."

"You sound like you're enjoying this insanity."

"I am, I am. It's good to get out in the woods, commune with nature. Move it, we don't have all night."

Cursing steadily under her breath, she followed me through the woods. I was glad we didn't have to be quiet. Standish stumbled and tripped over roots, thrashed around among branches, generally sounding like an elephant in a cornfield while I glided between trees, instinctively avoiding all the obstacles.

Before long, Standish was gasping for air, so I stopped for a breather. "Are you going to make it?" I asked sarcastically. "Not like strolling down Broadway, is it?"

"How much farther?" she wheezed as she leaned against a tree trunk.

"I don't know. I probably could've been there and back by now without you."

"I noticed. How come you're so good in the woods?"

"Just a country girl at heart. My great-grandfather was an Indian. I spent a lot of time in the country when I was a kid. I still hunt and fish when I have some free time. You ought to try a little healthy recreation now and then. Ready?"

"I guess."

We reached a clearing. "Wait here," I said. "If this is the right one, there should be a path leading to the cabin."

I walked around the clearing until I recognized the path I had entered this morning. I oriented myself and located the one that led to the cabin.

"Over here, Standish."

When the path widened, Standish moved up beside me. We both saw the cabin at the same time. A light shone through the window. We slid behind a tree and I flicked off my flash.

I whispered in her ear. "I didn't think anybody would be here."

"Do you have a gun?" she whispered back.

Surprised, I said, "No, but it's probably only the police."

"I doubt it—doesn't feel like the police." I heard the rustling of her clothes before she thrust a small gun into my hand. "You might need this," she said.

I handed her the flashlight. "Cover me from here while I sneak up and see if I can get a peek inside."

"Take care, Doyle, I can't find my way out of here alone."

I squeezed her arm. We were getting positively sentimental about each other.

Highly developed night vision and the faint glow from the window enabled me to cross the yard and skirt a hitching rail without any problems. I tiptoed onto the porch, where I flattened myself against the wall next to the window and listened. It was quiet. Too quiet. I inched my head closer to the window until I could just look in and see a wedge of floor, a chair arm, and boots. Boots! They were in a twisted position with feet in them. I looked squarely in the window. Now I could see half a body, the head and upper torso concealed by a couch. Instinct told me no one else was there.

"Standish, hurry." Impatiently, I waited by the window, staring at the feet. The boots looked familiar. Oh, hell, all boots look alike.

Standish peered over my shoulder. "Who is it?"

I shrugged. "Let's go see."

I tried the door and it opened. I let it swing inward while I stood to the side. Standish was just behind me and had her service revolver out. She stepped past me, crouched, and swung the gun around, covering all points of the room.

I followed her in and looked at the body. "It's Mrs. Thorne's groom," I said. I knelt beside him, felt his neck for a pulse, and looked up at Standish. "He's still warm."

"Don't touch anything," she said automatically. "Jesus, this is a nice kettle of fish. I have to report a body. What in hell am I going to tell the Nassau police? Here I am on a murder scene with a fugitive from justice. I knew I shouldn't have listened to you. What an idiot!" She slapped her forehead.

I had forgotten that the Nassau County police were looking for me. "No rush, Standish, let's have a look around. I'll take a peek out back."

What I found out back startled me. A road—a rough one, but passable even by an ordinary car this time of year when the ground was hard. I noticed a dark wet spot on the ground, stuck my finger in it, and sniffed. Oil. A car with an oil leak had stood here not too long ago. Brilliant detective work, Doyle, I mocked myself.

I went inside. "There's an old farm road out back. Probably goes back to the main house. Fresh oil on the ground. Whoever did this came by car. That should clear me. You'll make a terrific witness."

"If I'm not in the next cell," Standish muttered. Her face was anguished. She perched on the arm of a chair.

"Doyle, I'm going to do something I never thought I would." I waited expectantly while she searched for words, sorted out her ideas. "I'm going to break the law. I just can't think of any way to report this murder without getting both of us into so much trouble we'd never get out." Her eyes glinted angrily. "But you and I are going to solve this murder along with the general's and his wife's."

I patted her shoulder. "A wise decision, Standish. I know what it cost you. Now, let's really search. You've gone this far, you might as well go the rest of the way."

We searched professionally, carefully. No one would know we had been there. I found a packet of letters to Mrs. Thorne from somebody who signed just "J" and slipped them into my pocket.

We met in the living room. "What killed him?" I gestured at the body.

"Stabbed once in the heart. He had his jacket off. Whatever he was doing here, he was in no hurry. How did he get here?"

"Probably rode a horse."

"Where's the horse now?"

"Snug in its stall, I bet. Or maybe just turned loose. In which case, there should be a saddle around here. Did you see one?"

She shook her head. "Two stabbings and a shooting. Why not three stabbings or three shootings? Are they connected? coincidence?"

"Are you talking to me?"

"Just thinking out loud. I can't decide if we've got two cases or one. What do you think?"

"One," I said promptly, thinking that would distract her from our group.

I wandered into the bedroom and contemplated the chalk outline on the floor. Lydia Thorne's body had lain there not too long ago, I thought. Absently, I noted the rumpled bedspread. What had the groom been looking for? Did his murderer find it? Did the groom walk in on the murderer? Were they both looking for the letters? All kinds of questions. No answers. Crime of passion? Crime of money? I was thoroughly befuddled. I wished I was sitting quietly in my living room, drinking a glass of wine, and watching the Manhattan lights.

Standish called, "Don't you think we should get out of here?"

I reentered the living room. Scratching my head, I said, "I can't help but think we've missed something. Something obvious." I looked around the room. "I don't know what it could be," I said in disgust.

"Great." She headed for the door. "How do we find our way back?"

I laughed. "With this," I said, showing her the compass that I'd secretly consulted on the trip to the cabin. "Let's go."

"Some Indian," she scoffed.

The trip back to the car was uneventful. We drove to an all-night diner. Surprised to see it was already midnight, I called Jackie.

"They left a long time ago," she said. "They didn't have a search warrant. They want to talk to you. They think you murdered Mrs. Thorne. I told them they were crazy."

She sounded very calm. I was beginning to feel as though she was really my daughter. "Well, I didn't kill anybody, kiddo. I'll be home shortly. Why don't you go to bed."

Standish and I silently finished our coffee and headed back to Queens. We circled my block, looking for strange cars, then Standish parked in the alley. She left the motor running as she half turned to look at me. "It's been a weird night, Doyle. I'll talk to you tomorrow."

"Hey, don't worry about it. You did the right thing." I punched her lightly on the arm. "See you."

I watched her drive slowly away. Poor Standish, I thought, I was turning her life upside down.

Jackie was lying on the couch in my office, engrossed in an old Bogart film. I ruffled her hair and watched the movie for a minute before I said, "I think I'll take a shower. Then we can discuss the day."

"Hey, I'm glad you're back," she said softly without taking her eyes off the screen. "I was worried."

After I showered, I returned to the office and turned on the answering machine. One message: "I warned you. You went to see the old lady. I'm not sending you ten thousand. Watch out for your daughter. Last chance."

The whispering man. How'd he know I'd been to see Mrs. Thorne? Was I being watched? I glanced at Jackie, but she was still mesmerized by Bogart.

"Jackie, come here." Reluctantly, she left the couch. I said, "Listen to this," and hit the replay button.

She sat down. Her face paled. "What—what's he mean?"

"Obviously it's a threat. A new kind that I hadn't had to deal with before because you've been on the West Coast, out of sight, out of mind to this kind of vermin. Someone knows you're here. I just don't get it. Who could know I have a daughter, much less that you're here?"

I rubbed the bridge of my nose. My back ached. I was bone-tired. "I'm sorry, I just can't handle this right now. I'm dead. I'm going to bed. We'll discuss it tomorrow."

"You're not going to send me back to California, are you?" She looked at me anxiously.

I fiddled with the button on the machine while my brain replayed the message and I stared at my daughter—my beautiful, smart daughter. "I don't know. It might be best..." My voice faded and I shook my head. "See you in the morning."

EIGHT

Sunday Morning

A NOISE WOKE ME UP. A shadow lurked in the doorway.

"Who?" I struggled to see the figure.

"Mother?"

"Jackie?" I'd forgotten her again. "What's wrong?"

She walked over to my bed. "I didn't know if I should wake you or not, but that red light on your answering machine has been on for the past hour."

"Okay. What time is it?"

"About nine."

"Would you make me some coffee?"

After she left, I went to the bathroom and stared at myself in the mirror. Confirmed—I looked as bad as I felt. I could be at least ninety with these suitcases under my eyes. I splashed cold water on my face until I felt reasonably human.

Jackie handed me my coffee as I punched the machine into operation and sat down on the couch. Jackie perched on a nearby chair. I considered sending her out of the room but decided she might as well learn right now what life could be like in this madhouse.

Mrs. Thorne the Elder sounded like a vengeful angel.

"Who killed my daughter-in-law? Since you became involved, the situation has deteriorated. What are you doing about it? Call me."

I smiled at Jackie. "I wish I'd never heard of any of them."

Two social invitations made a nice change for the next messages. I made a mental note to call and regretfully decline.

The next caller had Standish's irritated voice. "You going to sleep all day? Nassau police called me around six. They've found the groom's body. Somebody tipped them. They'd like us to pick you up. I'll be over in a couple of hours. Run, fox, run."

"Another body?" Jackie's eyebrows lifted incredulously.

"Sounds like an epidemic, doesn't it? I'm beginning to feel like the Typhoid Mary of homicide. It was Mrs. Thorne's groom." I hesitated. "We found him last night in the cabin where she was murdered. For reasons I won't go into, we didn't report the crime. Incidentally, it goes without saying, I hope, that anything I tell you or anything you overhear is strictly confidential."

"Oh, Mother, I'm not a child. Besides, I watch detective shows all the time. I know how it goes."

"I hate to disillusion you, kiddo, but my life isn't exactly like a television series. I deal in real life, real death."

I pressed the button for the next message. Mary Ann said, "Good morning, Abby, just heard on the radio about the general's wife. Does that take our merry little band off the suspect list? Give me a call if you need help."

I drifted into a trance, letting my computer run. After a few minutes I dropped Mary Ann's card into the dialer.

"Mary Ann, Abby here. I need a sketch of that whole beach area, including a layout of the bunker and the roads and paths coming into the general area of the bunker. Pretend you're a bird-watcher or something. Can you do it?"

"Can do. I'm sure my husband has another full day of football lined up. I'll take the kids. They're always a good disguise."

"Fine. I'll stop by or send somebody to pick it up tonight. Have a nice day."

"Sounds like a TV commercial." She laughed. "See you later."

To Jackie, I explained, "Mary Ann teaches high-school art. Terrific artist. She's a member of the group. You'll like her. Earth-mother type. Unflappable." I pushed the button again. Nothing. "That's it. Let's have breakfast."

After breakfast I straightened up the apartment and Jackie watched me. Finally, she asked, "Aren't you leaving? I think Detective Standish meant for you to disappear. She'll be here soon."

I gave her my inscrutable smile. "I can't think of any place to run at the moment. Besides, I've got to do what's best for you."

"Does that mean you're quitting the case?"

"Nope."

She pouted. "Then it means you're sending me back to California."

"We'll discuss that—" The bell rang. "There's Standish now," I said, grateful for the interruption.

I checked the monitor before I released the elevator. Interesting, I thought, she's alone. I always thought cops went through life two by two. I was sure she was going to arrest me.

She entered the hall and snapped, "I thought you were smart enough to get my message."

"I got the message, but I have a problem." I led her into my office and played the threats from the whispering man. "Well, what do you think?" I asked Standish, who was staring moodily at the machine.

Standish glanced at Jackie. "I think we've got a problem." I was surprised and gratified to hear her use "we." She scratched her head. "She's as safe here as she would be anywhere. This place is impregnable, isn't it?"

"As far as I know. I'll show her all my little secrets." Jackie was watching both of us. I winked at her before I said to Standish, "I suppose you're going to take me to Nassau County now."

She jumped. "Oh, yeah, I'd almost forgotten. You have the right to remain silent—"

"I know the rest of it. Am I really under arrest?"

"Not exactly. They're mumbling about you being a material witness. They're fishing. If you'd talked to them last night, you'd be in the clear today—at least on the groom's death."

My eyebrows lifted. "They don't really suspect me of that one, do they?"

Standish blushed. "They did mention that they couldn't find you last night in the proper time span."

I shook my head. "But *we* know where I was, don't we?"

Standish looked miserable as she nodded.

"Standish, I like this case less and less. Would you be terribly upset if I said I didn't think the same person did all three. How about a two and one split? One incident is a red herring or an opportunistic murder. Like when you get a series of murders apparently done by the same person, but later you find one or more were committed to take advantage of the situation. I think that's what we've got here."

She drummed her fingers on the table. "Might be, might be. But where does the whisperer fit in? First, he's going to pay you to stay away from the general's murder, then he somehow finds out you're involved and says he's not going to pay you. Then he resorts to threats to get you off the case. Where does he fit? Is he the murderer?"

I smiled. "Maybe we're taking him too seriously. I often get nuts on cases I'm handling. You know the type. They keep police lines tied up with their nonsense—false leads, false information, false confessions. Maybe, this guy just wants to feel important.''

"Possible, but I think we'd better take him seriously for now. We have three bodies already." She glanced at Jackie. "I wouldn't want to add a fourth."

I followed her look. "You're right. We will act as if he's the real thing and hope he's just a prankster."

"Oh, by the way, that cigarette lighter had two identifiable prints—the general's and, I assume, yours."

I smacked myself on the forehead. "Dummy! I'm sorry, Standish. I didn't even think about fingerprints. When I found the lighter in his pocket, I assumed it was his. That's worse than the rankest amateur."

Standish grinned maliciously. "I'm glad to see something penetrate that ego of yours. Get your coat. Let's go." Standish and Jackie went into the living room, talking about what the detective called real police work.

I grabbed my jacket off the couch. It felt heavy. I found a packet of letters in the pocket. It took me a minute to remember they were from the cabin. I slid them under a cushion on the couch before I rejoined Standish.

"Handcuffs?" I stuck out my hands.

"Don't be ridiculous. Let's go."

"Keep everything locked up, Jackie. Don't let anybody in. Oh, let me show you the entrance into the factory." To Standish, I said, "I'll just be a minute. I want to make sure she's safe."

NINE

Sunday Afternoon

ANOTHER COLD DAY. Standish headed out Northern Boulevard. Traffic was light.

"Where're we going?" I asked.

"The cabin." Standish grinned. "This time, all the way by car."

I glanced in the sideview mirror. My computer flashed an alert. "We're being followed."

Standish checked her mirror. "You sure?"

"Yup. Black sedan now in right lane, three cars back. Two people in front seat. Hard to tell if male and female. That car has been in that same relative position for a long time. Pull over and stop."

Standish pulled onto the shoulder of the road and stopped. She faced me so it would look as if we were talking, leaving me in a position to inspect the car when it passed us.

"A man and a woman," I reported. "He looks like nothing you'd want to meet in a dark alley. She's young, fairly attractive. She averted her head when they got abreast of us. License plates obscured by dirt. Car is a sedan, dark blue, General Motors product, late model. Damn cars all look alike today." After Standish pulled back onto the road, I said, "Wonder how they're going to get behind us again without being obvious."

When we passed C. W. Post College, a dark sedan pulled out of the entrance. "There they are," Standish said. "Do we try to lose them or let them tag along?"

"Let them come. Maybe we can get our hands on them somewhere along the way."

"Or they'll get us," she grumbled.

"Standish, you're such a pessimist."

"And you're such a jerk. How in hell have you survived this long?"

"I'm superefficient. Beneath this happy-go-lucky exterior lurks an omniscient computer. Care to push a button and check it out?"

"Someday, someone is going to punch one of those buttons of yours and black out your computer permanently," she warned.

I laughed. "Not a chance. There's our turn up ahead. Hang a sharp left."

Standish spun the wheel, accelerating across two lanes of oncoming traffic amid much squealing of tires and honking of horns. I slid down into my seat, sure that any minute a car would hurtle into my lap.

She pulled safely into the lane leading to the Thorne farm and grinned at me. "Scared?"

"I'm always this shade of green. I didn't mean for you to commit suicide." I glanced out the back window. "That slowed them down a little."

"Oh, oh, trouble."

I looked to see what Standish was talking about. A car with two men standing beside it blocked the lane. My instincts told me they weren't Nassau's finest.

I glanced behind us. "We're surrounded."

"You wanted to get a hold of them. Well, take your pick, wise guy." Standish stopped the car. "Get the gun out of my ankle holster," she said.

I fumbled it out of its holster and slipped it into my jacket pocket. I was beginning to think of that gun as mine.

Standish rolled down the window and flashed her badge. "New York City Police. Clear the way, please."

"Very civilized," I muttered, never taking my eyes off the two walking up behind us. "Action, Standish."

"Keep calm. There may be a perfectly logical explanation for this."

"Marie Antoinette said that as she was sticking her head under the guillotine. Come on, come on, do something."

"I can't do something until they do something. I'm a police officer."

"Well, I'm not," I snapped as I pushed the door open and rolled out, ending in a crouch with my gun aimed at the two behind us. "Stop right there," I shouted. "Standish, watch the two in front."

"Stalemate," she whispered.

I glanced over my shoulder. One man was aiming a shotgun at Standish. There was no way I could shoot him before he nailed her. I looked at her sadly. "You could have ducked."

"Drop the gun," ordered the woman.

I did.

Time shifted into slow motion. What only took minutes seemed to last for hours.

It was four against two. I wondered about the chances of the Nassau police coming in or out. Didn't these people know the police were nearby? Did they care? Were they going to shoot us? Kidnap us?

"Put your hands on the steering wheel," said the shotgun toter to Standish. He shifted his position so we were both covered. I didn't enjoy looking down the barrel of that shotgun. Standish grasped the wheel so tightly that her knuckles were white. Her lips were in a thin, chiseled line and her eyes mere slits as she stared at the shotgun.

Since they made no effort to conceal their faces, I guessed we were in for a one-way trip to nowhere. Painfully, I thought about my daughter, how we were finally becoming close. I glanced at Standish, wondering if she had a family. We hadn't had time for personal conversation.

The woman, handing her gun to her partner, strutted toward me. Young, lithe, a panther stalking a mouse. Her dirty-blond hair framed a thin, angular face with opaque eyes.

"Hands behind your neck," she ordered.

She frisked me, but she missed what my hand could just barely touch, a knife in a sheath that I wore down my back when I expected trouble. I had been wearing it since the mysterious phone calls began.

The odds aren't right, I told myself, not with that shotgun pointed at Standish's head.

The blonde stepped away from me. "She's clean." She picked up my gun before she walked around the car, where she ordered Standish outside. She plucked Standish's .38 off the seat and laid both guns on the hood of the car before she ran her hands lightly over Standish.

She removed Standish's handcuffs from her belt and signaled me to come around the car. She cuffed us together. Then she stuck Standish's guns into her pockets.

I grinned wryly at Standish. "This is probably the closest we'll ever be."

"Shut up," she growled. "Where're you taking us?" she asked the woman.

"Later, cop. Harry, drop the cop's car at Howard Johnson's down the road."

She grabbed my free arm and led us back to her car, where she shoved us into the back seat. She sat in front. "Any sudden moves and I blow somebody's head off. Clear?" We nodded. "Okay, Max, let's go."

Standish said quietly, "We're supposed to be meeting the Nassau police right about now. If we don't show up, they're going to have an all-points out for us."

She laughed. "Ain't that cute, Max. They're worried about us."

I shifted my attention to Max. I shivered. His face was partially reflected in the rearview mirror. A purple puckered scar covered most of the right side of his face, twisting his lips into a perpetual sneer. His eyes were small black raisins embedded in sloppy folds of fat. His hands, splayed on the steering wheel, were at least three sizes too big for his height. He was about five nine, but had the hands of a giant linebacker. His right hand was also covered with the same type of scar tissue. He was every child's vision of a movie monster. I almost felt as if I knew him.

Miserably, I thought, I could pick either one of them out of a police lineup. I would have felt a lot more optimistic about our futures if they had blindfolded us. I glanced at Standish. She looked as calm as if she were being driven by the police commissioner's chauffeur.

My cuffed hand was falling asleep. I wriggled it.

Standish grinned at me. "Nervous, Doyle?"

"What'd you do, go to the Clint Eastwood school of acting for cops?"

"Wise guy."

"Cut the comedy, you two. Max doesn't like to be distracted when he's driving." She glanced at Max. "How much farther?"

He grunted. "Five, six miles."

We seemed to be headed for some place on Long Island Sound, not too far from the Thorne farm. It was an area of large, secluded estates. Nobody would be on the water either.

Max braked suddenly, throwing us forward as he turned into a lane. I missed the name on the mailbox. The road was dirt, rough, and rutted. After about a mile we came to a paved driveway, and Max pulled up in front of a sprawling white house that looked deserted. Shades covered the windows. The paint was chipped and peeling. Broken tree limbs and winter storm debris were scattered on the lawn and driveway.

"There it is, just like he told us it would be," the woman said. "Some place, eh, Max?"

Max grunted. "Yeh. Nice place. Get 'em out."

She opened the door and stepped back. I dragged Standish out. Standish swore as she barked her shin on the door. "Can't you watch where you're going," she growled.

"I'm not used to towing a trailer," I snapped. We grinned sheepishly, realizing we only had each other and time was running out.

For sheer entertainment the blonde gouged me in the ribs with her gun barrel. "Follow Max."

Max shuffled around the house. All the windows were covered. We waited while Max fiddled with the back door. I looked at Long Island Sound shimmering in the sunlight and wished I was out there sailing.

The lawn gently sloped down to the shore, where there was a large boat house and dock. On either side of the lawn a thick growth of conifers spread down to the high-tide line. We were completely isolated. Nobody could even see the house unless they approached by water or the lane out front.

My computer, working overtime, was overloading when Standish jerked the bracelets a little to get my attention. She nodded toward the two thugs who were arguing because Max couldn't pick the lock.

"Break it down," the woman ordered.

"Nah, he said leave no signs. I'll get it. Relax."

"We haven't got all day."

"That's done it." Max pushed the door open.

Standish muttered, "Can't win them all. Be cool."

"Move it." The woman gestured with her gun.

I was glad to be inside, out of the wind. My feet were freezing. The interior had the chill of a house whose furnace was set at the lowest point to prevent the pipes from freezing.

I glanced around. We were in a large kitchen laid out like a restaurant kitchen with an island in the middle, oversized ranges and refrigerators.

"Must have thrown some great parties," I said.

The woman giggled. "You're here for the last one."

Giggling seemed so out of character that Standish and I looked at each other in amazement—the same thought probably running through our minds—why was Miss Nasty so nervous?

Ignoring everybody, Max plodded through the kitchen into a hall with several closed doors. It was dark in this area.

He hesitated. "Let's take them upstairs," he said, opening a door that led to a narrow stairway.

Servants' quarters, I silently bet myself. "I'm disappointed," I drawled. "I did so want to see the grand ballroom, didn't you, Standish?" Standish looked at me as if I had just lost my marbles.

I was right behind Max on the stairs. He turned and casually swatted me on the side of the head. I reeled backward, but Standish propped me up as my ears rang.

"You okay?" Standish whispered. I nodded. "Keep your mouth shut. They're getting testy," she warned.

"Move it," the woman snarled.

At the top of the stairs we entered a hall where light streamed through a small round window. I glimpsed the Sound, so I knew we were still in the back part of the house.

Max opened and closed several doors. I wondered what he was looking for.

"This'll do," he grunted. "Inside."

I knew what he'd been looking for—a large storage room with no windows. A faint gleam of light from the hall revealed the bare dimensions—no furniture, nothing. When the door closed, it would be a black prison.

"Welcome to your future home," he said.

"For how long?" I asked.

He shrugged. "A while." He walked out.

"Don't try anything funny. Max and I'll be right downstairs," she warned. She closed the door.

It was dark. Black. Silent. After a few minutes I felt sensory deprivation or at least what I imagined to be sensory deprivation.

I was relieved to hear Standish whisper, "I think they've left. I think I heard a car."

I had almost forgotten we were attached, so wrapped up in the darkness had I been. "Now what do we do?" I asked.

Standish chuckled. "I think I unlock these cuffs and we take a nice hike in the country."

"You have a key?"

"You bet. When I was a rookie, I had a very embarrassing moment when a thief locked me up in my own cuffs. My partner, an old pro, told me to always carry an extra key hidden where I could reach it." I felt her fumbling around with her free hand. "Here it is."

A slight snick of the key and I realized I was free. Rubbing my wrist, I said, "Let's get out of here. Which way is the door?"

"Walk until you hit the wall, then follow it until you come to a door."

"How come you don't have a flashlight hidden on you?" I grumbled.

"I'll add that to my kidnap kit. Move."

We stood back to back before we marched off in opposite directions, looking for a wall. I banged into one first. "Got it."

"Great! Now find the door."

I inched along the wall, came to a corner, and started down the next wall. "I've got it," I said after going a few feet. "Where're you?"

"Opposite you. Keep talking."

I tried the door handle. It wouldn't budge. "Not going to be easy getting out of here," I said. "These old houses are really built." I tugged on the handle. I felt Standish's presence behind me. "I can't move it," I complained.

Her hand closed over mine on the doorknob. "Let me see if I can pick it." I listened to her fumbling around while my mind darted off in strange directions. "Ah, that did it," she said as the door swung open.

We listened and heard nothing. The house felt empty. "I think they've gone," I said.

"Let's go back to the kitchen."

We tiptoed down the hall to the stairway, where we paused to listen for a moment before descending. A strange sight awaited us in the kitchen.

"Do you see what I see?" Standish muttered.

"Yeh, but why?"

Cautiously, we approached the center counter. We stared at the guns.

"No apparent booby trap," she said before she picked them up and examined them. "Still loaded. They were so sure we couldn't escape they left them. Or maybe somebody's supposed to pick us up." She holstered them. "Want to take a look around?"

"Not much point to it. Besides, we have a long hike ahead of us." Outside, I took a deep breath as I stared at the Sound. Beautiful, blue sparkling water. "A fantastic place to live. Wonder who owns it?"

"Thinking of buying it?"

"No way." I laughed. "Let's go."

TEN

Later, Sunday Afternoon

WE TRUDGED DOWN the lane to the main road, where we looked for a car we could flag down. Nothing. We headed for Route 25. Beside me, Standish cursed the cold, the country, and the doubtful ancestry of our kidnappers, while my computer operated full tilt.

Finally, I said, "There was something strange about this whole incident, Standish."

"The strange thing is a walk in the country. I'm freezing. When I get my hands on those creeps, they're going to pay."

"I think to get your hands on them, you'll only have to find the right theater group or acting organization."

Standish stopped and stared at me. "What in hell are you rambling about? Actors!"

I grinned. "Seriously, Standish, have you ever seen a more inept pair of kidnappers? They don't search you very well. Or me, for that matter. They leave you in a room where you can pick the lock. They leave your guns in the kitchen. They leave you unblindfolded, so you can find your way back.

"Even the swat on my head was more theatrical than real. If he'd really wanted to injure me, he'd have used his gun barrel. And the dialogue. Really, Standish, right out a Grade-B movie. They let us see their faces. If we catch up to them—and knowing you, we probably will—I think the most serious charge will be malicious mischief. I don't even think their guns were loaded.''

Standish stamped her feet on the ground. "Geez, my feet are like ice.'' She stared at me, a perplexed look on her face as she thought about what I'd said. "Maybe, just maybe, you're right. But who hired them and why?''

I shrugged. "The murderer or one of the murderers or somebody who wants to muddy up the investigation. Somebody who has a pipeline into your office or the Nassau police or my office because the one with the shotgun was in place before we got there.''

"Huh?'' Standish raised an eyebrow. "Mind explaining that to me again?''

"Keep walking or we'll freeze to death.'' I took a deep breath. "Look, we don't know whether we're dealing with one, two, or three killers. And there are other reasons to put us out of commission for a few hours.''

"What other reasons?''

"Land,'' I said cryptically.

"You want to expand on that a little, Doyle?''

"Later. I don't want to confuse the issue more than it is. Besides, I need more facts.''

Standish eyed me suspiciously. "It occurs to me, Doyle, you could have masterminded this little charade yourself."

I shrugged. "I could have. But why?"

"To distract me from your merry little group, which I haven't thought about for some time now."

"Forget my people. I'd be very surprised if there was a killer among them."

I was disappointed. Standish and I had finally been getting some rapport, but now she was suspecting my friends and me again. I knew she was struggling to make some sense out of the morning's events, but I had credited her with more subtlety than she seemed to possess. I needed her on my side, but I didn't want to give the condo information yet.

Admit it, Doyle, I said to myself, you're just being selfish. You want to solve this all by yourself, collect a flat fee, and also get revenge on the one who had threatened your daughter and tried to set you up for a murder rap.

We trudged along with Standish still muttering imprecations while I silently thanked my little group for all the hikes we took during the year. I was actually enjoying the walk, but I didn't mention that to Standish.

Finally, we reached 25A. Watching cars whizzing by in both directions, Standish said gloomily, "Probably nobody will stop."

"They're certainly not going to stop if we just stand here doing nothing. Wave your badge."

She looked at me. "My badge?"

"Yeah, that ought to get somebody's attention."

It did. A pickup truck stopped, and the burly farmer looked suspiciously at Standish's badge. "New York City, eh?" Standish nodded. "Where ya goin'?" he asked.

"Howard Johnson's," I replied.

"Howard Johnson's!" Standish looked at me incredulously.

"Police car, remember? You're responsible for it."

She slapped her forehead. "I forgot."

The farmer dropped us off across the road from the restaurant and sped off before we could thank him. We darted across four lanes of traffic.

Standish scanned the parking lot. "There it is," she yelled.

"Coffee, first." I sprinted for the door.

"But the police are probably looking for us," Standish panted.

I smiled at her as I slid onto a counter stool and ordered two coffees. "You are the police, Standish. At least, the only one I care about. You could call and see if they're still waiting for us." I glanced at my watch. "We're almost four hours overdue." I ordered two cheeseburgers. Standish swallowed her impatience and ordered a corned beef on rye.

When she returned from the phone, she said, "They're upset. They'll meet us at the farm in half an hour. They thought you'd overpowered me and escaped."

"Fat chance," I said between bites. "I suppose they were going to shoot me on sight, except they don't know what I look like." I shook my head. "Cops," I added derisively.

"Watch your mouth, wise guy."

I relaxed. Our normal relationship—friendly antagonism—was back. And to think, there had been a point today when I had felt quite warmly toward Standish. Once a cop, always a cop.

We were halfway out the door when Standish asked, "Hadn't you better check on your daughter?"

"Good idea. She's probably worried." When Jackie answered, I asked, "Anything doing?"

"All quiet here. What's happening with you?"

"Tell you later. Check the answering machine."

She came back in a couple of minutes. She said, "A man called Ricky said he had something important, but he'd call you back because he didn't know where he'd be."

I thought about that before I said, "Take the other phone off silent ring. When it rings, pick it up. It will still be on record, but if you hear Ricky again, talk to him. Find out where I can reach him. Got that?" She repeated my instructions. "Okay, fine. Don't reveal your presence to anybody else. See you later."

I hoped Ricky wasn't doing anything stupid. Why hadn't he just left a message on the machine? He knew it was secure. I didn't like this. He had told me he couldn't get any more information until Monday. Now I had something else to worry about.

ELEVEN

Late Sunday Afternoon

WE DROVE TO the farm.

Two detectives were leaning against a car parked near the stables. Standish turned off the motor and opened her door. I grabbed her arm. "Hey, did you tell them anything about what caused our delay?"

She smirked at me. "Car trouble."

I grinned. "Good thinking."

Standish shook hands with the two cops, apologized for being so late, and introduced me. I could see that they were itching to search and cuff me but restrained themselves out of deference to Standish. After all, she didn't seem too concerned that I might be an unleashed mad-dog killer.

They ushered us into their car and drove to the cabin. The hard scrabble lane looped behind the barn and approached the cabin from the rear—just as I had guessed the night before. We drove through a large open field where a few horses drifted aimlessly, lifting their heads to watch us go by. I wondered what would happen to the farm now.

Woods surrounded the cabin on three sides. The cabin was bigger than it had seemed last night in the dark. A large brick chimney clung to the north wall.

Funny, I thought, I don't remember a fireplace. That caused me to doubt my powers of observation. There were two hitching rails in the back and a covered well near the north corner of the building.

Oddly enough, considering how immaculate the rest of the farm and its buildings were, there was something strangely unkempt about the cabin and its environs. No flowers—even in January, a flower bed would be discernible—no outline of a lawn of any kind, no amenities. Almost an unused air about the place, but the inside of the cabin belied that impression.

Lydia Thorne was beginning to interest me more now that she was dead. I regretted that I hadn't made more of an effort to talk to her when I had the chance.

Standish broke the silence. "Is this where the bodies were found?"

Detective Clark, the thin nervous one, answered, "Yes. The groom found Mrs. Thorne's body in the cabin." With a pointed look at me, he added, "After *she* was out here. Then, this morning we came looking for the groom, couldn't find him around the barns, so we drove out here. The lights were on. We found his body in the living room."

Clark stared at me. "We thought you might have been mad at the groom for what he told us, so naturally we wanted to talk to you. Very elusive you are, even when the NYPD has you in hand."

I smiled. "I don't like to go out early. Ruins my whole day," I drawled. "Besides, New York always has a budget crisis, and the condition they allow those police cars to get into, just unbelievable, eh, Detective Standish?'' The sentence was convoluted even for me, but it delayed Clark's thought processes. "May we see where you found the body?" I asked.

Clark led us inside while the other detective, Dombrosky, stayed in the car. I glanced at the chalk mark on the floor. I looked at Standish. Her expression was bland, unreadable. Like me, she realized the body had been moved since we saw it earlier. The chalk mark, outlining a small body in a fetal position, was now in front of the door. If it had been there last night, we wouldn't have been able to get in that way. Who had moved it? Why?

I was getting a headache.

Clark was staring at me. Standish was studying Clark. I was gazing into another world. The general preoccupies us, I thought, while Mrs. Thorne is only a divertissement, and the groom, dessert. *Cherchez la femme*. Is the general the red herring?

I yawned in Clark's face. "Very interesting, I'm sure. Now, do you mind if I leave? I've participated in your little charade. I'm bored. I'm tired, and frankly, I have more important things to do," I said as arrogantly as possible. Out of the corner of my eye, I saw Standish pale and gape at me in horror. I turned to her. "Really, Detective Standish, I just came along to humor you. Now, if there are no warrants or other trifles, I'd like to leave... *toot sweet*."

Clark flushed. "Now—now—wait —justa—"

"Do you have a warrant?"

"No—but—but—"

"No *buts*, Clark, drive me back to my car. I do not choose to play this stupid game." I swept out like a grande dame from the court of Louis XIV.

Standish caught up with me and in a vehement whisper demanded, "What in hell do you think you're doing?"

I winked. "Just follow my lead. Keep your mouth shut."

Sliding into the back seat, I snapped, "Home, James."

Still fuming, Clark slammed his door and nodded to Dombrosky.

When we arrived at Standish's car, Clark jumped out and shook his finger at me. "You haven't seen the last of me."

I smiled wearily. "Ta-ta, Mr. Clark. Bring a piece of paper next time. If you don't bother me for a couple days, I'll solve your silly little murders for you."

We drove away. I looked in the rearview mirror. Clark, practically jumping up and down, was screaming at his poor partner.

I grinned. "Our Mr. Clark gets rattled easily, doesn't he?"

With pity in her eyes, Standish looked at me and said, "You must have a death wish. If I were you, I wouldn't come to Nassau County for the next fifty years."

Standish dropped me off across the street from my place and drove off. I took a quick look around but didn't spot anybody who might be spying on me. I let myself in.

Jackie had the apartment door open. "I've been watching for you," she said. "I was worried. How'd it go?"

"Later." I patted her shoulder. "Make me a cup of coffee, please. I need a shower."

She returned to my room just as I was putting on my robe. As I combed my hair I could see her watching me in the mirror.

"Any important calls? Did Ricky call back?" I asked.

She set the coffee down near me. "No. Where've you been all day? I thought they'd arrested you."

I laughed. "They were just fishing. However, Standish and I were kidnapped for a while." I grinned at her horrified expression. "It was more like a Marx Brothers caper," I added, telling her about it.

She agreed with me. "They do sound like actors. What're you going to do about it?"

I sipped my coffee. "I'm not sure. I don't know if it's important to find them and I don't want to waste time on unnecessary maneuvers. If they're actors, I'm sure they were hired over the phone and paid anonymously. If not, they could be dangerous. Never underestimate the enemy. I think I'll leave them to Standish. Let's go listen to the machine."

I replayed Ricky's tape. "Abby, I found a real zinger. I have someone to see later. Then I may have an answer. I'll call you later. Don't try to call me. I don't know where I'll be or when I'll be back."

His voice was excited, panting as if he'd been running. Turning up the volume, I replayed the tape. Sounded like traffic noise in the background. I heard a voice of a passerby, speaking Spanish. I frowned. Spanish is spoken all over New York. A faint howl of a siren. A pay phone on the street? I had an uneasy feeling—he'd had lots of time to call me again.

Jackie said, "Maybe you should call him. His wife might know where he is."

"Not married."

"Oh?" Her *oh* said volumes.

"We're just friends. Ricky is perfectly sufficient unto himself. He's so involved with his causes and his birds that he doesn't think about companionship, male or female."

"What's he like?"

"A small man. Slender. Warm, friendly. A wee bit eccentric. Does flamenco steps to keep warm when he's waiting for buses. He's very organized, almost fussy. Prim. Dependable. Perhaps a little naive. He might not believe that something or somebody could be dangerous."

I thought about what I had said about Ricky. The last statement worried me. Ricky was apt to give everybody the benefit of the doubt except large corporations and the Corps of Engineers. Had he become suspicious of someone and approached him or her?

After a supper of soup and sandwiches—Jackie must think I never eat a regular meal—I went to my office to work on an efficiency problem for the next day. Jackie went to her room.

About ten, I laid down my pen, examined the flow chart one more time, and glared at the phone. I stood up and stretched before dialing Ricky's number and letting it ring several times. I couldn't think of any good reason why he shouldn't be home. Feeling uneasy, I removed my gun from the desk drawer before dressing to go out.

I tapped on Jackie's door and entered. "I'm going out for a while. The alarm system is on, the phone is on the answering machine. Don't read all night."

Her eyes were worried. "Where're you going?"

I smiled. "To see if I can find Ricky. Don't worry. He's probably hanging out in his neighborhood bar." I knew that was a lie since Ricky was famous for being a stay-at-home type.

Living with Jackie was like having an Irish mother around: Where you going? What're you doing? Be careful. I just wasn't used to sharing my life with someone else, and I hadn't had much time to think about it.

I'd always had an idealized view of motherhood—baking cookies, taking her to the zoo, exclaiming over good marks, buying her clothes. I was used to coming and going at my own pace without a thought to another living human being—or animal for that matter. Was I ready to share my life with Jackie day in, day out?

TWELVE

Sunday Night

RICKY LIVED ON the east side of Manhattan, almost directly across the river from me. He often ribbed me, saying he spied on me at night with his telescope. I usually retorted, "That must be as dull as bird-watching."

The doorman said he didn't know if Ricky was in but I was welcome to go upstairs, as he pocketed my twenty with a lascivious wink. Ricky's apartment was on the twentieth floor. I rang the bell. No answer. I debated for a moment. Then, after a glance at the television scanner at the end of the hall, I shielded the door with my body and picked the lock. So much for conscience when Big Brother is watching.

"Ricky," I called as I stepped inside. No answer. No sound except the gurgling of the fish-tank motor. I hit the light switch.

I crossed the large living room and looked out the window toward Queens. I grinned. The lights from my apartment stood out in that dark, desolate stretch. Just out of curiosity, I peered through the telescope. Wow! Details of my living room leaped into focus.

"That little devil wasn't kidding," I muttered. That set me to wondering how many other people focused on my living room. Residing in a deserted area with no high rises near me, I had always felt I had a lot of privacy. I shuddered. I didn't like the idea of a secret watcher, even a friend.

I looked around curiously. I had never been here before, since the group usually met in neutral locations. The apartment was typically Ricky—neat, organized. Beautiful enlarged photographs of birds and nature scenes hung on the walls.

I paused in front of the fifteen-foot fish tank that served as a divider between the living room and dining area. I watched the fish swim aimlessly around, lips pursed like officious bank tellers. There were exotic colors and patterns—purple, yellow, chartreuse, red, black, stripes, polka dots, fringes—nothing ordinary like a goldfish. A random thought—big fish eat little fish. LaChance was a big fish, Ricky a little one.

I wandered into his bedroom. Bed made. Nothing out of place. Cousteau's *Environmental Almanac* was open on the nightstand. I checked the closet, recognized the jacket he had worn New Year's Day.

In his den I searched for papers pertaining to LaChance. I studied the desk drawers, then tried a couple. Locked. I picked the locks. The papers concerned mostly business transactions or environmental issues. However, there was one surprise, a much-handled personal letter. I read it.

"Well, well, interesting," I muttered as I carefully replaced the letter. "Ricky has a son. He never even mentioned being married."

I searched my memory, recalling past conversations with Ricky. We never talked about anything except business or environmental issues. Did he ever mention any other friends? Where did he come from? Not New York; he had a trace of midwestern accent. His vacations revolved around trips offered by the American Littoral Society, the New York Zoological Society, and other organizations. His photographs on the walls commemorated these trips. I glanced at a photo of playful lion cubs and guessed that it came from his last vacation, a zoo photo safari to Africa.

I found his checkbook. Utilities, rent, health club, organization memberships, a few charities, stock purchases. Nothing really personal. None of those "to cash" that most of us have in our checkbooks. None to the local liquor store. His checkbook was as unrevealing as everything else about Ricky. When I really thought about it, I knew less about him than I did about most of our other group members.

I checked the rest of the apartment. The kitchen was neat. A saucer, cup, and small plate were in the drain. I even looked in the refrigerator. Depressing. Yogurt, a diet soda, milk, Brie, lettuce, tomatoes, carrots, and a carton of eggs. The bathroom was disgustingly neat too. No drugs heavier than Tylenol and cough drops.

It was discouraging. I wondered if Ricky was really this neat or if he had a zealous cleaning woman. I made one more circuit of the apartment before I shut off the lights and left.

I headed downtown to Ricky's office. Traffic was light. As I checked my rearview mirror I realized I was becoming paranoid. I navigated by the twin towers of the World Trade Center. Ricky's office was a few blocks from them in the financial district. They stabbed into the sky, beckoning me. Nobody was walking on the streets. A couple of winos huddled around a fire in a trash basket in an empty lot. A few cars cruised the area.

I parked the car across the street from Ricky's building, turned off the engine, and waited. A car slowed as it went by the corner. Was someone following me? A van turned up my street, drove by me, and turned right at the next corner. Catching a glimpse of a woman in the passenger seat, I chewed my knuckle. Did she really look like the woman who had kidnapped us, or was my imagination working overtime? I shifted the gun to my jacket pocket.

Familiar with entrance procedures, I nodded at the guard who let me in and strode to the sign-in book where I scrawled my name. I scanned the page. That's crazy, I thought.

"I see Mr. Carter is still here," I said to the elderly man minding the book.

He frowned at the book. He ran a dirty finger across the line next to Ricky's name. "He not been out all day."

"Anybody check to make sure he was all right?"

He shook his head.

On the tenth floor practically every door had a discreet gold script that said "Finch, Cochran & Case." I knew Ricky's office was a corner one. A faint light shone through a glass door. I smiled in relief. He's here, I thought as I pushed open the door.

"Hey, Ricky, I've been looking all over for..."

The office was a shambles, papers strewn all over, furniture tipped over, picture frames shattered. I moved from the secretary's room into Ricky's private office, where I found a repeat, only worse. Whoever had done this was in a hurry, no attempt at finesse or secrecy, just brute strength.

Standing in the doorway, I scanned the room, letting my computer register everything. Thank God, I thought, I don't see Ricky's body. With a sinking feeling, I crossed the room to a small bathroom whose door was ajar. I nudged the door and turned on the light. The room was empty. Spots of blood decorated the sink. I touched one. Dry.

I made a quick search of the office, knowing it was probably futile. Under the desk I found a bronze paperweight with dried blood on it and left it there. I sat on the edge of the desk, wondering what I should do.

Sighing, I called Standish, who grumbled about being awakened.

"I know Manhattan is a little out of your territory, but you'd better come over here. Remember Ricky Carter, the stock analyst? Well, he's missing, his office is a disaster, and there's blood here. He called and left me a message today that he had some important information."

Standish's voice was instantly alert. "Address? Wait there. Don't touch anything."

Slumped in Ricky's chair, I rummaged through my mind. The guard said Ricky hadn't been out all day. The phone call on my machine had obviously been made from an outside booth; ergo, there was a way to come and go undetected by the guards. That blood didn't necessarily have to be Ricky's. Someone could have broken into his office while he was out. He returned, saw the mess, panicked, and disappeared.

That's wishful thinking, Doyle, I admonished myself. Somebody had taken him away by force.

I wondered where he would have left me a message. I tried his dictaphone, empty. Telephone answering machine, empty. I looked more carefully at the papers in and around his desk, nothing. I had reached the height of frustration when I noticed Standish standing in the doorway.

She pointed her finger at me in a shooting motion. "If I had been a murderer, I could have nailed you easily. You're slipping, Doyle."

I nodded. "Cardinal sin of investigative work—never get personally involved." I rubbed my eyes and swallowed hard. "He's a nice man, Standish. A little guy who never hurt anybody. I shouldn't have asked him to help. If I had even dreamed there would be any danger, I wouldn't have."

Standish glanced away. "When you're through with the mea culpa, let me know and we'll get to work." She tapped her foot impatiently. "Hey, what was he doing for you?"

Recognizing the edge in her voice, I decided to level with her. "He was checking to see if the general was involved in any suspicious land deals or Corps decisions that would benefit somebody or a corporation."

"And was he?"

I decided to lie. "I don't know. Ricky said he'd get back to me and he didn't. That's why I came looking for him. I checked his apartment. It didn't look like he'd been there for some time, so I decided to check here and found this." I waved my hand as I watched Standish carefully, hoping she'd bought my little white lie. "He said it was difficult to check records on a holiday. He might have been here, just doing some of his regular work."

"He might have," Standish agreed, "but I doubt it. I think he was doing your research. I think you probably know more than you're telling me and I'm beginning to feel it's time to haul your tail down to the station house."

"Third degree?" I asked sarcastically.

Ignoring that, she asked, "Call the police yet?"

"You are the police."

"Local precinct, dummy." She picked up the phone and dialed. After a few minutes of cryptic conversation, she hung up. "They'll be here in a few minutes. I suggest you and I leave."

I raised my eyebrows. "I thought we'd have to hang around."

"I told them I had you well in hand, and that you couldn't have done it because you were with me." She shook her head. "I don't believe this. First, I don't report a crime—two crimes—now I dish out a phony alibi. If I keep hanging around with you, Doyle, I'm going to find myself becoming a master criminal or a candidate for the psycho ward. Let's get out of here."

THIRTEEN

Midnight

ON THE STREET Standish looked me over critically. "I guess you'll pass. There's a bar a few blocks from here—Reilly's, a cop bar. Meet me there. Try to act like one of *us.*"

From the outside Reilly's looked like the kind of place I'd pass by. The window was filthy, reducing the inside activity to a blur. I pushed the door open. Inside, it was hot, smoky and crowded. Men and women I assumed were cops jostled each other, shouting for the attention of the harassed barmaid, who, in turn, was watched by a portly Irishman perched on a stool next to the cash register.

Probably Reilly himself, I thought.

When my eyes adjusted to the haze, I noticed a morose-looking man sitting at the end of the bar. The others left a little space around him. He was staring into his half-empty glass of beer, seemingly unaware of the din around him. He looked vaguely familiar. I took two steps toward him before Standish called my name and snagged my arm. I hadn't noticed her half-hidden in a booth near the door.

I slid in across from her, my eyes still on the man. I asked, "Who's the somber guy at the end of the bar?"

She turned slightly to look. Her expression changed to a mixture of disgust and pity. "Used to be a cop. Name is Morgan. He and his partner went down a dark alley one night. He froze and his partner got his head blown off by a hopped-up teenager with a shotgun. The department never forgave him and he couldn't forgive himself, so he hit the bottle."

"What would you say if I told you he was following me earlier tonight? Probably picked me up somewhere around Ricky's apartment."

With renewed interest, Standish studied Morgan. Sneering, she said, "I have great respect for your powers of observation, but this time I think you've slipped a cog. He couldn't follow his own shadow in the shape he's in."

A gum-chewing waitress paused at our table. "Whaddyahave?"

"Two beers," I said. After she shuffled away, I said, "You trying to tell me he's an alcoholic?" Standish nodded. "Uh-uh, an alcoholic doesn't nurse a beer the way he's doing. And his eyes are just a little too alert for a drunk. When I came through that door, he spotted me all right, and he's been sneaking peeks in our direction ever since. Does he know you?"

"I doubt it. I joined the force after he'd been pensioned off."

"Was he here when you came in?"

Standish rubbed her eyes. She watched the waitress leave the beers on the table before she said, "I'm not sure. I spoke to a couple people I recognized before I sat down here." She shook her head in disgust and sipped her beer. "You know, Doyle, I don't think he *was* here."

"Did he walk by you when he came in?"

"You were the first one through that door after I sat down. But there is a back entrance for cops only—and he certainly would know about it—down that back hall where the rest rooms are. From the back alley, you'd have to know the door was there to find it."

"So, he saw us talking on the sidewalk. Guessed we were going to meet somewhere, followed you, lucked out when you picked this place. He entered through the back door. Piece of cake."

"But why?"

I shrugged. "I don't know, but I'm willing to find out."

I slid out of the booth and walked by the bar toward the rest rooms. Hunching over a little, I clutched my side as if in some pain. Once in the hallway, I glanced back. Morgan couldn't see me from where he was sitting. I slipped out the back door.

I picked my way through the debris in the alley. The immediate area consisted of short blocks of narrow, twisting streets, part of old New York. I trotted around the nearby streets until I found his car parked about a block away on Maiden Lane.

Panting, I leaned against it. "Certainly looks like the right one, Doyle." I laughed. "Better be." I smashed the window with the butt of my gun, unlocked the door, and pulled the hood release. I removed the distributor cap and closed the hood but left the door open to make it look as if some kid had attempted to steal the car. I memorized the license plate number. Returning to the alleyway outside the bar, I tossed the distributor into a dumpster and entered the cops' back door.

When I walked back into the bar, I noted the look of relief on Morgan's face before he turned back to his beer. He had been watching for me all right.

Standish glared at me. "You were in there a long time. I was beginning to worry about you and so was he."

I laughed. "I disabled his car. At least, I hope it was his car. It looked like the one that followed me earlier. He's going to panic when he loses us and he's going to need further instructions."

Standish shrugged. "I still think you're on the wrong trail. By the way, you do know you just committed a crime, don't you?"

"For a good cause." I studied the bar scene. Morgan didn't seem to exist for other people. Nobody spoke to him. I wondered how he'd felt when Standish led him to this place. Poor bastard—hard to live with the disdain of your peers, especially when you're a cop. Better to be a rogue cop than a cowardly one.

I glanced at my watch and gulped my beer. "Now!"

I stood up, leaned over, pretending to whisper something to Standish, and then, spinning on my heel, was out the door so fast, I bet Morgan was stunned. I sprinted to the corner and glanced back over my shoulder. No one had followed me out. I hid in a dark doorway across from Morgan's car.

A mangy cat rubbed against my leg, purring happily. "Go away," I hissed. Cat hair all over my good pants. It's a hard life, Doyle.

I didn't have to wait long. Morgan trotted up the street, then stopped and stared at his car. I took a good look at it too, and suppressed a giggle. Someone had come along and finished what I started. The tires were gone and the car was sitting on milk crates. New York strippers work fast. Morgan slammed his hand on the roof of his car and stared up the street. I followed his gaze. Standish was slowly, teasingly driving by the corner.

Morgan hurried down the street toward the bar. I visualized the hall again. The phones were across from the rest rooms. I gambled. I raced back to the alley entrance and darted into the women's room, where I leaned against the wall, gasping for breath. You're getting old, Doyle. I held the door slightly ajar so I could see the phone. Sure enough, Morgan appeared, dropped in a coin, and dialed. I couldn't see the number.

His voice was low, hoarse, causing me to miss words. "Lost...car...stripped...Doyle...what..." He listened. "Okay." He hung up and slipped out the back door.

Nuts, I thought, that wasn't too informative. Do I follow him on foot or get my car? I gave him a couple of minutes before going into the alley.

I glimpsed the arm coming down, but I didn't react fast enough.

The next thing I knew, a flashlight was shining in my eyes, I had a splitting headache, and I heard a gruff voice asking, "You all right?"

"Move the light, please." I could just make out the comforting blue uniform. "Somebody sapped me when I came out."

"Did you see him? You a cop?" another voice asked.

I shook my head. A mistake. Pain shot through the left side of my head. I pressed my head with both hands to keep my brains from falling out.

The cop with the flashlight said to his partner, "I think we'd better drive her to the hospital."

"Good idea," I agreed.

Morgan was long gone and I might have a concussion or worse. He'd dinged me pretty good. There'll be another round, Morgan, I promised myself. We'd underestimated him.

My visit to the hospital was uneventful. No concussion, just a big bruise on the left side of my forehead. I identified myself to the two officers, lied about the incident, and had them drive me back to my car by invoking Standish's name.

"Thanks, fellows," I called as they drove away.

Nice guys. I was sorry I couldn't give them anything to work with, but I didn't want Morgan arrested. I wanted him running fat and free.

Manhattan is no fun when you have a headache. I drove home. Standish had put the wheels in motion to find Ricky. The police had resources I didn't.

Jackie was asleep, curled up on the couch in the living room, a Nero Wolfe mystery open on her chest. I smiled.

Seeing my presence, she opened her eyes and stared at me. "What happened to you?" she gasped.

I touched my head gingerly. "This?" I smiled reassuringly. "Somebody hit me over the head. Nothing serious. He just wanted to slow me down and he certainly did."

Her face was pale, pinched. "I didn't..." She glanced away. "I didn't know there was any real danger. I thought you were exaggerating."

I sat down on the couch beside her and took her hand. "Jackie, maybe you'd better rethink your decision. As you can see, there are dangerous times in my life. When it was just myself, I didn't take them too seriously. Now I have to worry about you. I'm not sure I can handle it full time."

Jackie squeezed my hand. "I'll get used to it. Didn't you have to when you first started?" I nodded. "I really want to live with you. Maybe I can even help you sometimes."

I sighed. "First thing tomorrow I'm sending you to my friend, Rex Ayaya, an expert in self-defense. I want you able to take care of yourself. Rex has a pistol range and he'll teach you to handle a gun, too."

She shook her head. "Judo or karate is all right, but I don't like guns."

"I don't either. Humor me. I'm not telling you to pack one like Wyatt Earp. Just learn to shoot in case it's absolutely necessary. Someday, someone will come up with a workable, acceptable form of gun control and get them out of the hands of all the crazies, but until then, we're on our own."

She frowned at me. "But you seldom carry a gun."

"True. But I do know how to use it and I'm willing to use it if I have to. Think of shooting as a sport—New York's version of surfing."

She smiled. "I really think that comparison is reaching a little, don't you?"

I did my Groucho Marx. "Say the secret word and you get to go to bed. Now beat it."

I grabbed a cold beer from the refrigerator and went into my office, where I checked the answering machine. I returned Standish's call.

"Morgan returned to the bar, made a phone call in which he mentioned my name, but that's all I overheard," I told her. "Then I lost him. He suckered me. Must have known I was in the john. When I went into the alley, he sapped me. A couple cops took me to the hospital... I'm fine. Hard head. I lied to them. Said I didn't know who hit me. Anything on Ricky?"

"Nope. They're checking hospitals. I'll call if I hear anything." She paused. "Maybe you're right. Maybe Morgan's been faking. He doesn't seem to be in as bad shape as he pretends to be. I'm going to run a check on him." She yawned. "Well, tomorrow is another day."

"For you, it's another day. For me, it's hard work. I have to start an efficiency study in a chemical plant in Jersey. Keep me posted. Oh, by the way, I'm sending my daughter for instruction in judo and guns."

Standish laughed sardonically. "Does she wish she'd stayed a California beach girl?"

"Not my daughter. She'll be just fine."

FOURTEEN

Monday Morning

MONDAY DAWNED CLEAR and cold. A newsman on WCBS radio rehashed the murders, speculating about a love triangle. I laughed. Obviously the reporter had never seen the groom; a comic vision of the tall, elegant Lydia waltzing with the short, grizzled groom crossed my mind. That's the media. When in doubt, opt for romance, sex, sensationalism, which is easier than digging below the surface.

Digging reminded me of the Corps of Engineers, which led me to Ricky, which set me to wondering if he'd been found yet.

Jackie entered the kitchen, where I was waiting for my coffee to perk. I raised my eyebrows. "Morning, kiddo, short night?" I poured coffee for both of us. "By the way, someone from Rex's place will pick you up at ten."

"Do I really have to take shooting lessons?"

I frowned at her. How do you explain to your daughter that you're not a member of the National Rifle Club or a gun nut, but in certain professions a gun is a tool. Unfortunately, sometimes I had to suppress my liberal conscience and carry a gun. That lapse in ideology had even saved my life a couple times.

I poured a second cup of coffee. "Jackie, learning to shoot won't hurt you. You might even enjoy it. After all, it's an Olympic sport. I hope you live your life never having to fire a shot in anger. But, for now, humor me. Learn."

She shrugged. "I guess it wouldn't hurt. Do they supply the guns?"

"Yes. Now, let's discuss more pleasant things. Today I'm going to redesign an ancient chemical factory."

"How do you do that?"

"First, you burn down the building..." Her shocked look stopped me. I laughed. "Okay, seriously, you begin by studying its current mode of operation."

I was still describing my procedures when my secretary, Christopher Palmieri, arrived at eight.

Tall, slender, and impeccably dressed for a day in a Park Avenue office, he bowed when I introduced him to Jackie. "Charmed," he said. "You don't look much like your mother—fortunately."

"Chris, if I buy a couple more computers, you can be replaced. Let's go into the office. We have several things to discuss before I leave."

People might think I was playing role reversal or something, but of all the applicants for the job when my original secretary retired a few months ago, Chris was the best. Even though we are close in age and he is attractive, we maintain a purely professional relationship. Besides, he's married to my lawyer, Maria.

I gave him a synopsis of the weekend's adventures and played the tapes for him.

He steepled his fingers together and stared at me. "Sounds serious. Why didn't you call me? I could have come in."

"Thanks, Chris, but there was really nothing you could do." I gathered up papers and put them into my briefcase. "By the way, if Detective Standish calls, have her call me at the plant. I want to talk to her. And please keep an eye on Jackie."

ONCE I REACHED Erickson Chemical Company in Bayonne, I put the Thorne case out of my mind. I spent the morning interviewing department heads and key workers before I went onto the factory floor to watch the daily operation. Erickson was faced with the usual problem in a technically fast-changing world—modernize or close down.

By three o'clock I was presenting my preliminary findings to the company president, Al March. His secretary interrupted my report with a message. "A call for Ms. Doyle on four."

Standish's voice boomed, "I have good news and bad news. The good is we found Carter. The bad is he's in tough shape."

I closed my eyes. "Where'd you find him, and how bad is he?"

"In a car in the long-term parking lot at Kennedy. He's been beaten up—probably left for dead by his assailant. Doctor says fractured skull, broken left arm, left wrist, right ankle, possible internal injuries, lost a few teeth. In short, a mess, but he'll live.''

I envisioned Ricky as a bloody mess. Peaceful, bird-loving Ricky meeting up with some human animals, if you could call them that. More like a subspecies. I swallowed the bile rising in my throat. "What hospital?"

"Long Island Jewish."

"Nassau County? Why there?"

"Brain specialist."

"Anything new on the general?"

I happened to glance at March, who was watching me with the fascination usually reserved for rattle-snakes. I realized he probably didn't know about my second career. This conversation must seem a little ominous to him. I smiled weakly in response.

Standish said, "Nope. Nassau police haven't progressed on their two either. I'm beginning to think that wherever *you* go, disaster follows."

"Maybe. Look, can I call you when I get home? I'm in the middle of a conference. Thanks for calling." I hung up and slipped back into the persona of Abigail Doyle, Efficiency Expert.

AN HOUR LATER I was headed home, my heart aching for Ricky. I had to see him. I stayed on the Long Island Expressway and headed for the hospital on Lakeville Road.

At the reception desk I gave a spectacular hand-wringing impersonation of Ricky's sister since I knew only close relatives were allowed to visit a patient in intensive care. The receptionist gave me a pass.

A nurse in the intensive care unit looked at the pass and then at me. Dubiously, she said, "You don't look much like him."

"How can you tell? I understand his face is smashed."

She pursed her lips. "True. Follow me, please." She stopped at the foot of his bed. "Five minutes," she warned as she left.

Blinking back tears, I shut down my emotions. I didn't have time now for sentiment. Ricky looked ghastly, his face a swollen black-and-blue caricature of his normally neat features. He looked tiny in the bed, swathed in bandages and encased in casts.

Leaning over him, I grasped his unbandaged right hand. "Ricky, can you hear me?" No response. "Squeeze my hand if you understand me."

A long moment, then a barely perceptible squeeze. What could I ask him that would provide me with useful information from hand squeezing?

"Did a man do this?" Squeeze. "Was he alone? With a woman? Another man?" Squeeze. "Did you recognize them? Did you find out more about LaChance?" Squeeze. "Is the information in your office? At home?" Squeeze. "Papers? Tapes?" Squeeze.

"Time's up, honey," the nurse said from behind me.

"When can I visit him again?"

She shrugged. "Check with his doctor."

"Who's his doctor?"

She consulted the chart. "Dr. Mulvey."

I looked back through the window at Ricky and promised silently, "I'll get them, Ricky. They'll pay for this."

I bought a cup of tasteless coffee from a vending machine and went looking for Dr. Mulvey. I caught up with him in his office, where he was preparing to go home.

"I'm Ricky Carter's sister, Abby Doyle. Is he going to be all right?"

Dr. Mulvey was short and rotund, with beautiful, spatulate fingers. His eyes were kind, weary. He repeated the same list of injuries that Standish had given me.

He sighed. "He'll be here awhile, but I think he'll recover fully. He'll need some dental work and some physical therapy for the arm and leg injuries. I hope there's no permanent brain damage. He was hammered pretty good. Still, I expect we can move him out of intensive care in a few days."

"That's good, doctor. When will he be able to talk to me?"

"Tomorrow. Maybe." He was a doctor who obviously hedged his bets. "What he needs now is rest."

"Dr. Mulvey, I hope you don't take this the wrong way, but I'm sending a private guard to keep an eye on him."

He raised his eyebrows. "Is he in danger?"

I outlined the Thorne case, adding, "You saw him. He has information that somebody else wants or at the very least doesn't want him to pass along. I'd just feel better if he was well protected. I'll have a guard here within an hour. Is there someone I should clear this with?"

"I'll take care of it." He picked up the phone and I turned to go. "Mrs. Doyle." I paused, my hand on the doorknob. "You're not his sister, are you?"

I sighed. "Right now I'm the closest thing he's got to a relative in this world, doctor. He's a loner." He nodded.

I closed the door behind me. The doctor was all right.

I headed home after automatically checking in my mirror for followers. I had this premonition of danger, this feeling that I was being watched; but I didn't spot anything out of the ordinary.

"Paranoia will get ya, Doyle," I muttered wearily as I circled my block before I pulled into the alley and parked.

I looked across the river at the Manhattan skyline. Usually the sight lifted my spirits, but not today.

FIFTEEN

Monday Night

CHRIS WAS WAITING in the office for me. I glanced at my watch. It was six-thirty. "Am I paying you overtime?" I asked with a weary smile.

"You look whipped," he said as he poured me a glass of Beaujolais. "I just thought I'd hang around until you got home. I didn't want to leave Jackie alone."

"You're a gem, Chris." I sipped the wine. "I just came from seeing Ricky. Horrible. Which reminds me, arrange a twenty-four-hour guard for him. I've cleared it with the hospital."

When Chris hung up from making those arrangements, I asked him, "What do you think, Chris? Money? Woman? Revenge? What's the answer to our current soap opera?"

He fiddled with his pencil. "I made some calls today. Do you realize just how high society Mrs. Thorne is?"

"The mother or the wife?"

"Both, but especially the general's mother. She's so important that she pays a press agent to keep her out of the society columns. A friend of mine at *Forbes* magazine said she's among the top fifteen richest women—make that people—in the United States.''

I straightened up in my chair and kicked my computer into gear. ''Then why would her son need extra money? It wouldn't make sense for him to sell out to some corporation since his mother could buy and sell most of them.''

''If people only did things that made sense, you'd be out of business, Abby. Ever hear of greed?''

''True. You can never be too thin or too rich.'' I emptied my briefcase on Chris's desk. ''We have until Friday to finish the Erickson proposal. You can start on this mess tomorrow.''

He made a note on a pad on his desk. ''Do you want me to hire a bodyguard for Jackie? I listened to those tapes.''

I shook my head. ''I don't think that's serious. Probably part of the game being run on me, part of that loony kidnapping.'' I had second thoughts, but I suppressed them. It was difficult to admit I couldn't protect my own daughter.

''Tomorrow, do a complete check on General Thorne. I want everything right down to his favorite brand of underwear. Keep Maria up to date, too, in case I need a lawyer in a hurry.''

I joined Jackie in the kitchen, where she was whipping up cheese omelets. Must be she was tired of sandwich and pizza menus.

''How was your day?'' she asked as I slid onto a stool.

"So-so. That chemical plant is not to be believed. It must have been obsolete at least ten years ago. I don't know why the owner waited so long to call for help."

"Chris said your friend Ricky was in the hospital."

"Did he say why?"

"No." She slid my omelet onto a plate and sat it in front of me. "An accident?"

"Hardly. He was nearly beaten to death." I noted the horrified expression on her face. "Now you see why I want you to take self-defense lessons. This can be a dangerous world, kiddo." I ate silently for a few minutes. "How'd your day go?" I asked.

She laughed reluctantly. "I must admit it was interesting. I picked up a few bruises from my first judo lesson. I didn't actually shoot a gun today, but we went over the different kinds of handguns, their effectiveness, how to take care of them, and so on. Next time it's the range."

"When's your next session?"

"Wednesday. He's booked tomorrow with some special group."

AFTER DINNER I tried to reach Standish. She wasn't at home or her office and nobody seemed to know where she was. I paced the floor, listening with half a mind as Jackie regaled me with stories of her college adventures. An hour later I tried Standish again with the same result. I couldn't wait any longer.

"Jackie, I have to go out for a while. Will you be all right?"

"Sure." She looked at me curiously. "Where're you going?"

"Ricky left something for me in his apartment. It might be very important."

AFTER CHANGING into black slacks, a turtleneck sweater, and a black windbreaker, I went into my office to get my gun. Jackie entered just as I was dropping it into my pocket and her face paled.

"Do you think you'll need that?" she asked.

"Never know. Don't worry about it. If Standish calls, tell her to meet me at Ricky's apartment. The address is on the pad by the phone." I ruffled her hair. "Don't let anybody in unless you recognize them. Call Chris if you need anything."

She frowned. "You aren't going to find any more bodies, are you?"

I laughed. "I certainly hope not. I don't want to try Standish's patience any further. See you later."

SIXTEEN

Later Monday Night

RICKY'S DOORMAN, remembering either me or my twenty, hastened to open the door. "Terrible thing about po' Mr. Carter," he said, shaking his head dolefully.

"Yes, yes, it was. I'm here to pick up some things for him." I was at the elevator before I remembered to ask, "Has anybody else been around asking about him?"

"No, ma'am."

RICKY'S APARTMENT looked untouched. I headed for his den, where I had seen a tape machine. There was no tape in it. "I wonder where he put it," I muttered.

After an hour's search I gave up and went to the kitchen for a glass of water. Leaning against a computer, I studied the kitchen while my computer ran, trying to retrieve a fact.

Ah, yes. On one of our canoe trips we had all been sitting around a campfire talking about mysteries, especially where to hide things. Ricky had mentioned a secret drawer in his kitchen.

Kitchen! Of course, dummy, it's here in front of your nose. I racked my brain, but I couldn't remember if he'd said exactly where in the kitchen that drawer might be. I groaned. Ricky had an absolute fetish about drawer space and the kitchen was no exception.

Where to start? Well, Doyle, just start.

I examined drawer after drawer and was halfway around the kitchen when I hit one that had a funny sound. I studied it. I was convinced this was the right one but couldn't figure out how to spring the secret compartment.

"Forgive me, Ricky," I mumbled as I took a hammer and chisel from his toolbox and smashed my way into the drawer, revealing a secret one behind, and in it was the tape.

After all that exertion, I rewarded myself with another glass of water and took the tape into the den. Ordinarily, I would have smiled at Ricky's melodramatic opening, but the image of him in that hospital bed was still too vivid.

"If you're listening to this tape alone, then something has happened to me."

I listened to the whole tape and frowned. Mary Ann or somebody had said, "*Cherchez la femme*," and she was almost right, except it was "look for the man" this time.

The tape answered the question of how a seemingly wealthy general could be bought by a large company; but he hadn't been bought, he'd been blackmailed. He had probably been afraid his homosexuality would cost him his military career.

I sighed. At that echelon it probably would have meant no more than a quiet little request to retire. Oh, but his mother! I could just imagine Mrs. Thorne's reaction. She would brook no disgrace to the Army. I wouldn't have wanted to be in the general's shoes when she got through with him. I suppressed a giggle as I envisioned that big, self-important man humbled by his little mother.

Suddenly it dawned on me that I had just heard a muffled sound somewhere in the apartment. A door opening? As I pushed the chair back to get up, the lights went out. I froze, then instinct took over. I dived under the desk, tugging at my gun, and crouched there, listening intently. I was beginning to feel foolish. It was probably just a blown fuse. My knee throbbed with arthritic pain. I couldn't hold this position much longer.

Someone banged into a piece of furniture in the living room. A muffled curse followed. Blood pumped in my ears as my blood pressure leaped. I eased my leg into a more comfortable position.

Where is he?

The darkness and the silence were unsettling. Flashes of Ricky in his bed came to mind, and I wondered if I was going to be beaten too. I tightened my grip on the gun. Whoever was in the apartment was taking his time, stalking me and enjoying it.

I mentally gauged the distance from my hiding place to the front door. Could I make it? Was he between me and there?

I heard another light sound, a footstep. I was tempted to peg a couple of shots through the den door. Another footstep. He was in the doorway. I raised my gun and aimed.

Bang. Bang. Somebody was hammering on the apartment door. I lowered my gun.

"Doyle, Doyle, are you in there? Open up."

Standish! I never thought I'd be so glad to hear her voice.

"Next time, Doyle," a muffled voice said from the doorway, "stay out of this or you die." A sound of shuffling, then silence.

"In here," I yelled to Standish. "Careful, some-one's in the apartment." I had great faith in Standish's lockpicking skill.

Her voice came from the entrance hall. "Stay where you are, Doyle."

I crawled around the desk, leaned my back against it, and stretched my legs out straight. What a relief! I hoped it was Standish I heard in the kitchen. The lights came on. I walked into the living room, where I met her coming from the kitchen.

She grinned at me. "Circuit breaker. You okay?"

"Thanks to you. Let's look around." We checked every room, finding no sign of the invader. I shook my head angrily. "Damn, how'd he get away?"

"He didn't pass me, so he must have left through the fire door that opens out of the kitchen. Mind telling me what's going on?"

I told her about the whispered threat before I played the tape. Standish sat on the edge of the desk, idly swinging one leg as she listened to the tape. When it ended, she asked, "Where does that leave us? We know why, but we don't know who. And how do Mrs. Thorne—the wife—and her groom fit into this?"

"She probably knew about her husband's preferences, and it was a case of you-go-your-way I'll-go-mine as long as appearances are upheld." She paused. "And who does Morgan work for? More questions. When do the answers come?"

I was more perplexed than ever. Ricky's tape was really short on details. It didn't point me in the direction of anyone who might have felt it necessary to kill Ricky. It didn't tell me if there was a jealous lover in the general's life. His wife's jealous lover? Why the charade of death in a military bunker? Nice touch, but did it mean anything? The tape also didn't give me any revealing information about LaChance.

"Curiouser and curiouser, as Alice in Wonderland might say," I muttered. "I think it's time to smoke LaChance out."

"Are you planning something stupid or something dangerous?"

"Both." I grinned. On a piece of paper I scrawled, "Don't bother messing up the apartment. I found the tape." I placed the note on top of the desk.

"Maybe this will preserve Ricky's apartment and his life."

"And put yours on the line." She grimaced. "Doyle, I don't know whether to admire you for your courage or pity you for your quixotic nature."

"You should be happy that I'm taking this case seriously. Come on, I'll buy you a beer. There's nothing more we can do tonight."

WHEN I GOT HOME, I replayed the threats I had received. The voice on the tapes and the one I heard in Ricky's apartment could have been the same; then again, distortion of taped voices made it difficult to be sure. I shrugged. Maybe I had met my nemesis.

I called the hospital and spoke to my guard. "Has Mr. Carter regained consciousness yet?"

"Not really. He mumbles a little, seems restless. Nurse says that's normal."

"Anyone call about him or try to see him? Any strangers hanging around the area?"

"Nope. All's quiet."

After I hung up I prowled around the apartment, testing my alarm devices, double-checking the locks, and mentally reviewing my precautions regarding Jackie. I peeked into her room. She was sound asleep.

I stood at the window, staring across at Ricky's building, wondering if a stranger was standing at Ricky's telescope staring back at me.

I went to bed, where I continued to stare, into the darkness now, seeing the ghost of a dead general. Did his mother know he was gay—or to be technical, bisexual?

SEVENTEEN

Tuesday Morning

I HAD JUST finished dictating the improvements for the Jersey factory when the doorbell rang and Chris left the room.

He returned with a whimsical smile. "I think you've been drafted. There's a man outside with enough brass on him to sink a battleship. Shall I let him in?"

Absently I said, "Might as well. Otherwise he'll shoot down the door."

A few minutes later Chris, wearing his best poker face, returned to announce General Ritter.

I stood up and extended my hand. "General, won't you sit down, please."

We stared at each other. He was gorgeous. Perfectly tailored uniform. Four gleaming stars. Chest full of medals. Iron gray hair. Ramrod straight, tall. Beautiful blue eyes. He must have been in his sixties but looked at least ten years younger.

Clean Army living, I thought.

"Do you have a tape machine running?" he asked.

I smiled. "Of course, General."

"Turn it off, please."

Glancing at Chris, I nodded. "Your move, General," I said, leaning back in my chair, forcing myself to relax. God, but he was impressive.

"I understand General Thorne's mother retained you to investigate his death. There'll be no further need of your services. The Army has taken over the investigation." He slid an envelope onto my desk. "Mrs. Thorne sends you this letter of dismissal and a check."

I smiled, leaving the envelope untouched. "I'm afraid you're too late, General."

His eyes narrowed, and the geniality faded from them. He was very much the commanding officer.

"What do you mean, Miss Doyle?" He bit off each word.

"I've learned quite a lot about General Thorne. I'm sure the police have too, and the newspapers probably aren't far behind." I glanced meaningfully at the envelope. "Just what did you want concealed—that he was a homosexual or that he was selling out to a large construction company?"

The general blushed.

Interesting, I thought, I didn't think generals did anything so human. What embarrassed him the most, I wondered—corruption or sex?

He stiffened. "Can you prove either of those accusations?"

"Both," I said blandly, glancing toward Chris at his desk, seemingly engrossed in a stack of papers. "Now, if you'll excuse me, General, Mr. Palmieri will show you out."

I hated to send him away. I just wanted to sit there all day and feast my eyes on him. What a prime example of American manhood. All those medals. Courage. Intelligence. God, he was handsome. I wish we could have met in other circumstances.

He stood. He was just a shade this side of apoplexy. "You haven't seen the last of me," he threatened. He pivoted.

"General," I called softly. He turned. "You forgot this."

He snatched the envelope from my hand and marched out of the room. Chris winked at me and hustled after him.

Chris returned, touched his tie, and said, "The general was in a high dudgeon. Don't you love that word?"

"Nice word, but we have more important things to do than discuss language. We need to know who was blackmailing General Thorne and we need to know his contact in the LaChance company."

Chris sat in the chair recently vacated by General Ritter and looked thoughtful. "I doubt that General Thorne would have gone prowling through gay bars or subway rest rooms for companionship."

I smiled. "Some of our representatives in Washington did just that. Let's not rule out any behavior, no matter how bizarre or stupid we might think it is." I winced. "Was that sentence as convoluted as I think it was?"

Chris laughed. "You're beginning to sound like a general. I have a friend who might help us. He's a police officer and, incidentally, gay."

"Call him."

I signed letters while Chris was on the phone. Suddenly I was aware of a silence and glanced up. Chris was staring at me. "He knows the general," he said.

"Did he know Thorne personally or professionally?"

Chris shook his head. "You don't understand. Not Thorne. He knows General Ritter."

I groaned. "Don't tell me he's gay too."

"I don't think so, but Monty has seen General Ritter meeting another man in a gay bar in the Village. He knows it was him because they met when General Ritter had a car accident. The other man sounds like Thorne, but Monty thinks it was more in the nature of business than sex."

"Perfect. What better place for two generals to meet when they are up to no good professionally and financially? How many Army and business types hang around in gay bars?" I rubbed my forehead. "If they were spotted, the spotter would jump to the obvious conclusion—romantic tryst."

My head ached. My computer had accessed an excess of generals. I paced around the room. Chris busied himself at his desk, knowing better than to interrupt me.

I stopped at his desk. "Get Mrs. Thorne on the phone," I said.

MRS. THORNE'S VOICE wasn't as strong as I remembered it. A quaver gave her away when she answered my question. "Yes, I authorized General Ritter to terminate your employment."

"Because of what I've found out about your son's business dealings or his sex life?" I asked, mentally castigating myself for cruelty to old ladies.

A swift intake of breath and the iron was back. "You have your nerve, Ms. Doyle, to slander my dead son. I asked you to find his murderer, not malign him. You are fired."

"Wait, Mrs. Thorne, don't hang up. You can fire me, but you can't stop my investigation. There's still the matter of people in my group being suspects, including myself. I'm not quitting until I get all the answers. And, if you fire me, you won't be entitled to information about my findings."

She thought that over. "I won't fire you on one condition—anything you find comes to me first."

I agreed. Before she hung up, I quickly added, "By the way, do you think Lydia's death and your son's are connected?"

"I don't know. Haven't you got any leads on her murder?"

"I wasn't aware I had been hired to investigate that too."

"I—yes."

"Then I may have a lead. Did she know someone well whose name began with the letter J?"

"You mean did she have a lover whose name began with J?" The acerbic tone was back and I was glad. I preferred the iron lady I'd met earlier. "Yes," she snapped.

"Yes?"

"His name is Jay Farnsworth. He's an engineer of some sort. I believe the general introduced them at a party a couple years ago. He's also a horseman, and in case you hadn't guessed, the way to Lydia's heart was through her horses."

"Your son didn't care for horses?"

"He could take them or leave them, mostly the latter."

"Who inherits the farm?"

"I imagine Roxanne, their daughter. Before you ask, she's a captain in the Army, stationed at the Pentagon. She's very bright and dedicated to her career. Some observers predict she'll become a general in spite of not being a West Point graduate. Unfortunately, the Point wasn't open to women when she went to college."

"Does she live on her Army salary?"

Mrs. Thorne laughed sarcastically. "Of course not. But she's discreet about it. Nothing ostentatious, just comfortable. Since she doesn't fraternize too much with equal or lower ranks, there's no reason they'd get jealous." Mrs. Thorne paused before adding, "There's a lot of jealousy in the Army."

I thought about that. Maybe I'd been blinded by the obvious in General Thorne's case. "Were there Army people who were jealous of your son?"

"Of course. He came from a long line of generals and was preordained to become one himself. He was given excellent assignments and help from those above him who were indebted to the family in one way or another. He had money and social standing. Who wouldn't resent someone like that? Remember a lot of those young men—and now young women—at the Point are farmers' sons, shopkeepers' children. What do they know about the family tradition and life of someone like my son?"

"Did the general ever mention any fellow officer he had problems with?"

She snorted. "General Ritter."

I frowned. "Why did you allow him to fire me?"

"He came here and convinced me that not only was it for the good of the family and Roxanne's career, but also for the good of the Army."

"And maybe, most of all for the good of General Ritter," I muttered. "I'll get back to you. If you hear from Ritter or anybody connected to the Army, call me. If I'm not here, leave a message. And, Mrs. Thorne—don't trust anybody."

I hung up. Chris raised his eyebrows. "Well?"

"We have a couple of new players. Jay Farnsworth—probably Mrs. Thorne's mysterious lover—and General Thorne's daughter, Captain Roxanne

Thorne, U.S. Army, Pentagon. Make a discreet check of her whereabouts this past weekend."

He made some notes on a pad. "Why the daughter? Isn't that a little farfetched?"

I shrugged. "Children have killed parents before. Leave no stone unturned in this family. Was she Daddy's little girl or Mommy's?"

While Chris made several phone calls, I finished up some routine work. He hung up and looked over at me with a raised eyebrow.

"What did you find out about Roxanne?" I asked.

"Straight arrow, climbing fast in the Army due to a combination of family connections and natural talent for military strategy. Quiet private life, has had an affair, non-live-in type with the same man for ten years. He's a professor at Georgetown. She owns a house in Georgetown a couple blocks from his. She spends part of every leave with her grandmother and at least one weekend a month. She and the old lady are close. Roxanne and her father had a cordial but cool relationship. They also associated professionally at the Pentagon even though they were in different agencies. She and her mother shared a love of horses and rode together frequently, sometimes at the farm and sometimes at a mutual friend's estate in Virginia. Although the family doesn't appear to be one of those warm hug-and-kiss types, there doesn't seem to be any serious problems either."

"Then I can take her off the suspect list."

Chris frowned. "Well, there is one little thing. She's been staying with the an old friend in Manhattan since New Year's Eve."

"Funny her grandmother didn't mention that. Still, from what you say, I can't see Roxanne killing her father or her mother. As soon as I have some spare time, I'd like to talk to her. Keep track of her whereabouts."

"Do we pass any of this along to Detective Standish?"

"Not yet." I smiled at him. "Don't give me that accusatory stare. I know we promised cooperation, but what have we really got—a few rumors."

EIGHTEEN

Tuesday Afternoon

PUTTING THE CASE ASIDE, Chris and I concentrated on clearing up the backlog of work connected with my consulting business. Aching shoulder muscles finally broke my concentration.

Watching me stretch, Chris asked, "Are we skipping lunch? It's almost one."

"Where'd the time go? Let's rustle up some sandwiches."

"Jackie, lunch," I called as I walked through the living room on my way to the kitchen. No answer. I glanced into her bedroom. She wasn't there.

Chris called from the kitchen. "Jackie left a note here. Says she's gone for a self-defense lesson."

I stared at the note. "That's impossible. Rex is booked for today." I looked at Chris, silently begging him to disagree with what I was thinking. "No," I whispered as Chris headed for the answering machine.

Gnawing my lower lip, I listened to a voice I'd heard before—only this time instead of whispering ominously, he spoke in an upbeat tone. "Hey, Jackie this is Mike at Rex's. He says he can give you an extra lesson this morning. Had a cancellation. Why don't you get your mother to drive you over?'' Then, Jackie's voice. "She's busy. I'll take a cab."

Chris called Rex. "Damn," he said. "Nobody from his place called here. Now what?"

I sighed. "We wait. Call Standish and get her over here. Tell her nothing. I'll make some sandwiches."

On automatic pilot, I made a stack of ham sandwiches, adding ham, mayonnaise, and lettuce to slice after slice of bread as my mind recalled memories of Jackie. Jackie at three, Jackie at ten in the courtroom, Jackie on holidays, and finally the young woman I was just getting to know. Jackie—too trusting to see the danger in a simple phone call.

I berated myself. How had we missed that call? It must have come in on the other line while I was talking to Mrs. Thorne.

Chris placed his hand over mine. "Hey, that's enough sandwiches for the whole force. Standish is on her way."

I counted the sandwiches spread all over the counter—ten—and laughed uncertainly. "I eat a lot when I'm scared." I bit my lip. "Oh, Chris, I've never had to face this before. Why didn't I send her back to California after the first threat?"

Chris got two beers, shoved one into my hand, and sat down on a stool at the counter. "She'll be all right. They just want a temporary club to hold over your head. Remember that kidnapping farce they pulled on Standish and you?"

I shook my head. "Not the same thing, Chris. Those characters have nothing in common with this guy. I'm afraid he's the real McCoy. They were actors."

Standish arrived, morose and annoyed. "What's the harebrained scheme of the day?" she snapped, accepting a beer and a sandwich from Chris, who was convinced that the way to any cop's heart was through her stomach.

"Jackie's been kidnapped," I said, keeping my eyes on her face.

Her expression didn't change as she chewed on her sandwich, and I wondered if she'd heard me.

She tilted her head and looked at me suspiciously. "Is this for real or another one of your tricks?" She studied my face. "For real," she answered her own question. She glanced at Chris. "Any message from the kidnapper?"

He led her into the other room, where he replayed Jackie's conversation. I could hear the murmur of their voices, but I wasn't really interested. It no longer seemed to have anything to do with me. I stared at the refrigerator as a dull, lethargic cloud settled over my brain. I couldn't remember ever feeling this way; most cases, even ones with setbacks, were challenges to me. This time I just wanted to go to bed and pull the covers over my head. The old ostrich syndrome.

"Feeling sorry for yourself, Doyle?" Standish asked sarcastically. She leaned against the doorjamb, glaring at me. "Want to give up? Now that it's gotten messy, you scream for the police. What's the matter? Nobody offer you a hundred grand to retrieve your own kid? Tsk, tsk."

I flushed. I jumped up and took a couple of steps toward her, rage pounding at my temples. I wanted to wipe that sneer off her face. A slight smile curled her lips and she nodded to herself.

I realized she had been goading me back to action. "Close, Standish, real close. I almost ripped your face off." We grinned at each other. "What did you think of the voice?"

"Chris played all the messages. I think you're right, same man every time." She picked up a sandwich and separated the slices of bread to peer at the contents. She sighed. "We have three murders, one assault, one or two kidnappings, miscellaneous misdemeanors, and where are we? Nowhere."

She chewed on her sandwich while we stared at her. Finally she said, "There are red herrings and more red herrings in this case. Eliminate those and we'll be closer to finding your daughter." She raised an eyebrow at me. "Money or passion?"

"Money," I said promptly. I glanced at Chris, who nodded agreement.

Standish brushed some crumbs off her blazer. "There's nothing I can do here. Call me at the office if you hear from the kidnapper. I'm going to hassle the Pentagon for a while."

Pentagon rang a bell. I told her about General Ritter's visit. This time I leveled with her, telling her almost all that I knew, reserving only my conversation with Mrs. Thorne.

She grinned. "Two generals are better than one. If anything goes wrong, I'll be walking a beat on Staten Island. See you later."

I paced around the kitchen. "Chris, we need help. And who better than the gang that's been involved since the beginning." I told him to track them down and get them here as soon as possible.

Poor Ricky, I thought, how he'd love this.

I called the hospital. A nurse said he was improving and might even be able to talk a little later. My guard reported no problems.

Mary Ann was the first to arrive. She dropped her coat on my couch. "Boy, did my principal flip. I told him it was an emergency and he'd have to cope without me." She gave her irrepressible grin. "Now, what's so important. Are we all going to jail?"

"Jackie's been kidnapped," I blurted.

"Oh—I'm so sorry." She hugged me. "We'll find her."

Jill arrived next with her two youngest in tow. "I couldn't find a sitter."

I took them into my bedroom and plunked them down in front of the television set.

Debbie arrived with a handsome young man. His West Point ring told me this must be John, the Corps of Engineers fellow. "We were just going out," she said apologetically as she introduced him.

I shook his hand. "It's all right, Debbie. Maybe John can help. My daughter has been kidnapped. The Army's involved in this case. He can give us some fresh thinking."

"I'll try," he said in a deep, self-assured voice.

After Bob arrived I related all of the events leading to Jackie's kidnapping. Then I described every possible suspect to Mary Ann, who dashed off sketches of them.

I looked at the drawings, shaking my head in admiration. "I don't know how you do it. It's almost like having photographs of these creeps."

I passed the sketches to Debbie. "How about John and you canvassing the neighborhood to see if anyone saw any of these people in the area today."

We brainstormed for a while. Chris brought in some coffee and sandwiches.

Jill sighed. "I wish we'd never gone near that bunker."

Bunker! It had started in the bunker; could it end in the bunker? Would they hold Jackie there? Deserted. Isolated. Not many people walking the beaches in this weather. Limited access.

"What're you thinking about?" Bob asked.

I smiled. A shark's smile. "That bunker. I think I'll pay it another visit."

"Now?" Chris asked.

"Tonight." I looked at my friends. "I don't know what I'd do without you guys."

Bob grinned. "After all, we're suspects too." His expression turned grim. "Besides, it's dirty pool to take your kid."

Mary Ann drew a map of the area around the bunker, and the group voted to act as a support team. I felt better, knowing the wild dogs would have a choice of meals this time. We agreed to meet at my apartment just after dark. Everybody except Chris went home or back to work, whichever their consciences dictated.

Chris busied himself in the kitchen picking up the debris. He laughed. "I never thought all those sandwiches would disappear." He looked at me contritely. "Sorry."

I grasped his shoulder. "Chris, life doesn't stop. Humor doesn't disappear. You don't have to walk around here like you're at a wake. Everything will be fine."

I walked into my bedroom. "Oh, no," I groaned. Jill's kids were asleep on my bed. I dialed her number. "Forget something, Jill?"

"Oh, my God! Mike would never forgive me if I lost them." She chuckled. "I'll be right over."

After Jill retrieved her children, I took a nap, resolutely pushing Jackie to the back of my mind. I'd need all my strength for tonight.

NINETEEN

Tuesday Night

THE ALARM WOKE me at six. I thought of Jackie and prayed she was all right. Physically, I felt better, but mentally and emotionally, I was still functioning at half speed.

Chris greeted me with a cup of coffee. "No calls," he said.

I sipped my coffee. "I've been thinking about Mrs. Thorne. She might be in danger too. Send a couple guards out there. Call and tell her they're coming. Check with the hospital. Then you can go home."

Chris grinned. "And miss all the excitement? No thanks. I'll set up a command center here. Oh, Debbie and John got one possible on the sketches."

"Morgan?"

"How'd you guess? A waitress in the diner near the subway station said he was in there for coffee early this morning."

"Did she noticed what he was driving?"

"Nope."

"Did you tell Standish?"

"Yes. She'll be here shortly. Are you going to tell her where you're going?"

I shrugged. "Probably better for her career if I don't."

I went to Jackie's room, where I sat down on her bed and looked around the room.

She hasn't been here long enough to make this her own, I thought. No pictures, no posters. What is she doing now? Is she scared? Injured? Dead? I shuddered.

I heard Standish's voice and hurried back to the living room, where she was standing, gazing out the window. I stopped, nonplused. This was a Standish I had never seen before. A panther. Dressed in black, she glided across the room to stand in front of me, an enigmatic expression in her eyes. It dawned on me that she was way ahead of me, had read my mind, and was prepared to risk everything to join in my madness.

"You know?" I asked.

"I guessed. The bunker is as logical as anything else in this cockamamie case. Anyway, I came properly dressed for outdoor activities this time."

She sat down on the couch and stared at the skyline. "Don't get your hopes up," she said softly. "I don't think our kidnapper would be so foolish as to hold her in that bunker. Too uncomfortable and no way to protect himself in there." She nodded toward the window. "My guess is she's over there."

Reluctantly, my eyes were drawn toward Manhattan. The bunker seemed so simple, so accessible, while Manhattan was almost impossible. Where would we start if she was in Manhattan?

"Wherever she is, I'll find her," I promised.

After everybody arrived, we discussed the final logistics of our attack on the bunker.

"Be very careful of those wild dogs," I warned as they trooped out, leaving Standish and me to follow in my car.

We gave them a twenty-minute start so they could get into their assigned positions before we parked at the beach community. The night was dark, cold, and gloomy—a night to be home by the fire.

Bob, our first contact, was surf-casting on the beach. We picked out his form in the dark—reflections dancing around the dim lantern sitting near his feet—and hunkered down in the darkness behind him.

Pitching my voice above the rumble of the surf, I asked, "See or hear anything?"

He knelt, pretending to check his watch in the light. "Nothing. When I arrived, I saw a light way down the beach. Probably another fisherman."

"Okay. Catch you on the way back. Good fishing."

"You too."

We cut inland, relieved to get out of the wind blasting off the ocean. Traveling in the dark was tough, but I didn't dare use a light. I trusted my computer. Standish stumbled. I grabbed her arm and whispered in her ear.

"Careful. Hang on to me and make as little noise as possible."

Suddenly the shadows shifted in front of me. I gasped, but it was only the murky outline of the bunker breaking up the darkness. I touched Standish's arm.

"We're here," I whispered.

I knew the others would be in their assigned locations by now, ready to back us up. Debbie and John, pretending to be young lovers, were parked on the road coming in from the fort. I hoped they wouldn't get carried away with their roles and forget to keep watch. Mary Ann and Jill were on top of another large bunker just inland from us. Its elevation gave them a clear view of the whole area, and they had my night glasses. I assumed they were tracking us right now.

I placed Standish's hand on the wall of the bunker. "Follow the wall around until you come to the entrance. I'll find the other one. Allow five minutes before you go inside."

Standish pulled my head close to her lips. "For God's sake, Doyle, don't shoot me by mistake."

At the entrance I paused to listen. I wasn't prepared for the shot and the swearing that came from the other side of the bunker. I scuttled inside and flattened myself against the wall. I listened again, my heart thumping against my rib cage as my grip tightened on my gun.

I heard the muted sound of the wind and dripping of water somewhere to my left. I turned on my flashlight and played the beam slowly over the walls. There was Standish, gun in hand, staring into a room off the main passage. Shaking her head, she glanced toward my light.

In a surprisingly normal voice she said, "Come on down."

I joined her.

"I just killed a damn dog," she said. "He jumped me as soon as I came in. I overreacted."

"No harm done, Standish. My wild guess was wrong. Jackie isn't here."

Jill and Mary Ann raced into the bunker. "You guys all right?" Mary Ann gasped. "We heard shots."

"Another dog," I grumbled. "No one is here. It doesn't look like anyone's been here either."

A few minutes later Bob, Debbie, and John converged on the bunker. "We heard a shot," they said simultaneously.

"Just a dog," I said. "Let's meet back at my apartment. We could all use some coffee."

CHRIS LOOKED AT ME questioningly when we trooped into the apartment, cold, tired and disheartened.

I shook my head. "How about some coffee, Chris."

"No one said it was going to be easy," Standish snarled as she looked at our downcast faces. "If you did real police work, Doyle, you'd know it's a lot of tedious slogging, not just flights of fancy and lucky guesses." The sneer in her voice was palpable. We stared at her. "Fancy little group of do-gooders. Could use some real help from some real cops, couldn't you? Amateurs!'' She stalked into the kitchen.

Stunned, we grinned sheepishly at each other.

Chris was the first to recover. "I think Detective Standish is upset with herself, but I also think she's partially right. We just don't have the manpower to go it alone." He looked at me apologetically.

"It's okay, Chris." I hated to admit weakness. I gnawed my lower lip. "You're both right." I raised my voice. "Standish, quit raiding my refrigerator and come back in here."

She returned and glared at me suspiciously. I smiled at her. "As usual, you're right," I said. "We've lost sight of the real case, which is the murder of the general. Someone wants me to drop the case, so they kidnapped my daughter. Unaccustomed to being a mother, I went into a tailspin and ran around in circles, the reaction they were hoping for. Right, Standish?"

She nodded.

"Okay, I'm back on track now. There's nothing I can do about Jackie, so there's no point in spinning my wheels. I'm returning to what I do best. Chris, give Standish a picture of Jackie and let her start every cop in the city looking. The rest of you—go home, get a good night's sleep, and we'll see what tomorrow brings."

Mary Ann crossed the room and hugged me. "Are you sure this is the way you want it?" she asked softly. I nodded.

They left. I heard Standish and Chris talking in the office. I slumped on the couch, my head in my hands, my thoughts a jumble.

"Ahem."

I glanced up. Standish was holding a large photograph of Jackie. I stared at it. Her high-school-graduation picture. Would there be a college-graduation photo?

"I have to ask you a couple questions about your daughter," she said formally.

I waved a hand in assent.

"Does she have any scars or birthmarks?"

I realized that I hadn't been close to my daughter in so long that I couldn't answer that question. "I don't know," I said helplessly. "I don't know."

"Height? Weight?"

"About five seven, one twenty, one thirty."

"Age?"

"Eighteen—no, nineteen. Just beginning..."

"What was she wearing?"

I shook my head. "I didn't see her leave and I don't know her clothes that well." I gave her a pleading look.

She nodded. "Guess that's it for tonight. Go to bed. Don't go haring off on your own again." She gripped my shoulder. "What I said, I meant, but I didn't have to be that blunt about it. You need help, and sometimes you have to be bludgeoned into taking it. We'll treat her as a missing person and I'll give a false name to keep the press away from you. Incidentally, if

Morgan took her, she'll be all right. I don't think he'd kill a girl. Good night.''

When she reached the door, I called, "Hey, Standish, thanks.''

She flipped me a wave and left.

Quite a woman, I thought, quite a cop.

I entered the office, where Chris was talking on the phone, wearily running his hand through his hair. It was one of the few times I had ever seen him looking less than impeccable. His hair was messed up, his tie loosened.

He hung up. "That was Ricky's guard. Ricky is in and out of consciousness. Mumbles, but nothing intelligible. Nobody has tried to see him." He sighed. "No other messages. Would you like me to stay the night to man the phones or just keep you company?''

"No, I'll curl up on the couch here and leave the phones on. I'll just catnap." I rubbed my eyes. "Funny, isn't it—you don't realize how much your kid means to you until there's a possibility you'll never see her again.''

Chris gave me a quick hug. I touched his hand, grateful for his loyalty and his strength. "I'm sure she'll be all right," he said. "After all, she has a lot of her mother in her. She's probably scheming to escape right now.''

I forced a smile. "Be that as it may, we all need some sleep. Go home. Ask Maria to stand by tomorrow in case we need cash or her advice in a hurry.''

TWENTY

Early Wednesday Morning

My ALARM WOKE me at three. A bizarre thought flicked across my mind: I'm going to kidnap a general.

General Ritter still bothered me. He was an unknown factor. Where did he fit in? His demeanor and his anxiousness to remove me from the investigation had piqued my curiosity. His appearance at my office had been too coincidental with Jackie's kidnapping. How did the kidnapper know I'd be so preoccupied that Jackie wouldn't want to disturb me? I had a lot of questions for the general.

Monty had supplied me with General Ritter's Manhattan address, Sutton Place. Generals certainly lived well. Are the rich so altruistic that they want to serve their country, or do they get rich after they become generals? Some of them even become presidents.

As I entered the factory I whistled to Apollo, who padded along as I walked through to the back entrance. I didn't dare take my car in case someone was watching it. I caught the subway at Vernon and Jackson, a couple of blocks from my apartment, selected an empty car, sat down, leaned my head against the wall, and prepared to doze for the short time it would take to get to Grand Central Station.

The door between the cars clicked. A strong draft of cold air ruffled my hair, and I opened my eyes. Terrific, Doyle, I thought, just what you need, as I examined the three young toughs who were practically licking their chops at the vision of a lone middle-aged woman on the train.

I could tell they were predators, one white and two black males in their late teens, shuffling toward me, leering and jive-talking among themselves. In no hurry.

I watched them through half-opened eyes.

One of the blacks with a shiny gold tooth and a deformed right ear planted himself in front of me and leaned close, wearing a menacing smile. "Hey, Mama, what's happenin'?"

I smiled and jabbed at his eyes with my fingers. He reeled backward, screaming in shock. I jumped to my feet and pulled my gun. "Still wanta play, fellas?"

"Hey, lady, we meant no harm. Just teasing," the white guy mumbled, backing away, spreading his hands to indicate no weapon.

"Strip," I ordered, waving the gun.

Three sets of eyes opened wide. "What you mean?" one asked.

"I mean get your clothes off in a hurry. Everything but your shorts." I waved the gun and barked, "Now."

I smiled as I watched the bravado drain out of them and embarrassment set in as they hastily shed their clothes.

The train pulled into Grand Central. "Out," I ordered and herded them onto the platform.

"But our clothes," the white guy moaned as the train door shut and the train pulled out of the station.

"Have a nice evening, boys," I replied, and headed for the exit.

I DECIDED TO WALK uptown to clear the cobwebs out of my head. After the exhilaration of my victory over the muggers, I felt let down as the lack of sleep caught up with me.

I spotted a cruising police car, and, to avoid questions, I ducked into one of Bloomingdale's doorways. The cops drove by. Fondly, I patted Bloomie's stone wall. Although I didn't patronize it much, I realized it was a necessary institution for many of the city's rich and near-rich, if not to buy, at least to see and be seen.

I jogged toward the lights of the Queensboro Bridge and turned right on Sutton Place, slowing down to read the numbers. I found the general's building eventually, a monolith of stone and glass, probably with a terrific view of Queens.

Huddling in a doorway across the street, I watched the security guard behind a desk in the lobby. Frequently, he glanced at a bank of television screens behind him. He also watched the front door, which was unattended; either the doorman had gone off duty at midnight or was on a break. As I watched, another guard emerged from an elevator, paused at the desk to talk briefly, then disappeared down a hall.

No good, I thought.

I crossed the street and walked to the rear of the building, where I located a closed garage entrance, probably controlled by an electronic device. Also no good unless someone came home while I was standing there, an unlikely possibility even in the city that never sleeps.

I located the service entrance, which looked more promising. A discreet sign said *Ring for entrance*, so I did.

"Forget your key again, Melon?" a black man said as he opened the door. His eyes widened when he saw me. "You aren't..."

I pushed him backward and pointed my gun at his chest. "Just relax and everything will be fine. On the floor, face down, hands behind your back."

I cuffed him and straightened up to examine the entryway. No television scanner. "Chink in their armor," I murmured. Who was Melon and what would he do if he rang and didn't get an answer? Dismissing Melon as a real threat, I dragged the night porter back into his little room, where I stuffed a rag into his mouth and locked him in a closet. I unplugged his phone and hid it behind a stack of newspapers.

Wonder how much they'd pay me to burglar-proof this building, I thought, and considered ways of improving the system while I rode the service elevator to the twentieth floor. I crawled out of the elevator and sat, back against the wall, while I scanned the ceiling and walls to locate the cameras and figure the angles that would allow me to reach the general's door undetected. I had already deactivated the elevator to make sure it was ready when I was.

I weaved my way to General Ritter's door. Still in a crouch, I picked his lock and opened the door just wide enough to slither through. Standing up, hearing alert, I explored the wall until I found a light switch and turned it on.

Nice, I thought. The general lives well. Classy prints and paintings on the wall. A few pieces of Steuben glass scattered artfully on the tables and shelves. A collection of lead toy soldiers in a locked glassfront cabinet. A tasteful mounting of several photographs of General Ritter with Presidents Nixon, Ford, and Carter, and other military and civilian dignitaries. Impressive.

After a brief survey of the hall and living room, I started looking for the general's bedroom. My first guess turned out to be a guest room. I cracked the next door open and listened.

Snoring. Jackpot. I hit the light switch.

The general was a heavy sleeper. He slept on his back. Even asleep, he was handsome. I kicked a chair, and he woke up.

Unmoving, he stared at me. "What in hell are you doing here?" he asked after what seemed like hours.

I sat down on the chair I had just kicked. "My daughter has been kidnapped," I said conversationally. "I'm contacting everybody who might have a vested interest in her disappearance and my subsequent withdrawal from the Thorne case."

"You're mad." He hitched himself up in bed and looked at the clock. "Do you know what time it is?"

I smiled. "Of course. I suppose it's a little past the fashionable hour for calling on Sutton Place, but I do so hate crowds and my days seem to be rather busy."

I was beginning to feel like Alice in Wonderland having a conversation with a mad general. I was also having second thoughts. He didn't act like a man with anything to hide. Except—he had neglected one reaction. My computer told me his logical response should have included "that's too bad" and "when was your daughter kidnapped?"

"What do you want with me?" he asked.

"Well, let's just say that I'm willing to trade you for my daughter. Now, why don't you get dressed or would you prefer to be taken out of here in your pajamas?" I leered at him.

He flushed. "You're insane if you expect me to get dressed in front of you," he sputtered.

I sighed. "General, I'm sure you can satisfy your modesty and my determination to keep an eye on you by dressing with your back turned. I promise not to molest you."

In better circumstances, I wouldn't make that promise. He was gorgeous without clothes.

General Ritter's back spoke volumes, indignation in every rigid line, but strangely, no fear. Either he figured he had nothing to fear from me or he really had a clear conscience.

As soon as he dressed, I marched him out. "Walk naturally and don't try any cute signals for the cameras. We're going down in the service elevator."

He leaned against the wall of the elevator car. We stared at each other while I wondered what I was going to do with him now that I had him. We reached the basement and the door opened. I glanced out. "Let's go, General."

Suddenly I felt really dumb. Here I was, kidnapping a general, but how was I to get him home? By subway? Ridiculous.

"Uh, do you have a car, General?"

He smirked at me. "No. The Army provides a car and driver when I need one."

I nodded. "Figures." Taxi? Too risky. I sighed. "In here, General." I motioned him to sit on the cot in the porter's room. I opened the door, unlocked the cuffs, and rolled the man over. "Don't say a word. This is a security test. If you're lucky, I won't tell how easy it was to get by you. Don't ever open that door for Melon again." I glared at the man as I pulled the rag out of his mouth. "Understand?"

"Yesss."

"Let's go, General," I said nonchalantly, and steered him back to the elevator. "Let's go back to your place, have a cup of coffee, and talk this over."

THE GENERAL REGARDED ME as if I were an escapee from a lunatic asylum. He cleared his throat. "Good idea, Miss Doyle. Maybe you can explain your temporary insanity satisfactorily enough so I won't have to notify the authorities."

"You have children, General?"

"Two daughters."

"Then I think you'll understand my behavior." I finished my coffee and my story simultaneously.

"I think we have a fundamental misunderstanding here," the general said as he poured more coffee for me. "I would never harm your daughter. I had nothing to do with her disappearance. My only concern was to protect the Army. I never liked Thorne. We attended the Academy together, and he was a disgrace to the uniform. I can even explain that meeting in the village. An example of Thorne's warped sense of humor, forcing me to meet him in a place like that. I had confronted him about one of his shady business deals—"

"The LaChance thing," I interjected.

"LaChance? No. It was a large condo project in Florida that required dredging mangrove swamps. The swamps serve as a nursery for marine species. Obviously, a permit shouldn't have been issued since the dredging would seriously damage the shellfish industry. There was also danger from hurricanes, unsafe building practices, and so forth. A bad project from start to finish. The district officer had decided to deny the permit. Thorne interfered in the process, so the district officer asked for my help."

"And did you help?"

"I tried. I called Thorne and asked for a meeting with him. He picked the time and the place. Diabolical man. He laughed at me. Said I was now compromised, that he'd had a friend photograph me entering that gay bar."

General Ritter shook his head, his eyes flashing angrily. "What a devious mind that man had. I really assumed his wife had killed him or at least arranged it, so I wasn't too concerned at first. When she was killed, I didn't know what to think. I was afraid the picture might surface, that I might even become a suspect. I was frightened."

Although it was hard for me to imagine the general being frightened by anything, I believed him, because I now knew that we all have weaknesses. My daughter had proven to be my Achilles' heel.

I thought about what he'd told me. I was no closer to finding Jackie, but I'd eliminated one suspect and confirmed that General Thorne had been a wheeler-dealer.

The first rays of the sun crept into the general's kitchen. I was bone tired. Standing up, I extended my hand. "Can we be friends, General? Will you forgive me for my predawn shenanigans?"

He smiled wearily. "I'm afraid, Miss Doyle, that you and I are stubborn people when it comes to protecting the things we love. We've both made mistakes. If I can be of any service, please call me." We shook hands. "Let me get you a cab. You're a little conspicuous in your cat-burglar outfit."

We laughed.

"Incidentally," he added, "I'll see that the porter doesn't mention your little raid."

"Thanks."

As I left his apartment I promised myself that after this case was over, I would call the general and invite him out to dinner to make amends for my boorishness. Who you kidding, Doyle? You just want to get that gorgeous general alone again—under better circumstances.

TWENTY-ONE

Wednesday Morning

I DRAGGED MY aching body into my apartment and bumped into Chris, who was carrying a cup of coffee toward the office. He raised his eyebrows at my menacing and bedraggled appearance.

"What're you doing here at this hour?" I asked.

He traded me the coffee for my jacket and gingerly pulled out the .38. Chris didn't like guns. "I thought you might do something drastic," he said. "Did this help?"

"Sort of," I said, grinning sheepishly. "Let me get off my feet and I'll tell you the tale of the idiot and the general. Anything on the recorder?"

"Nothing."

I stretched out on the office couch while I told Chris about my meeting with General Ritter. "I guess he's innocent of everything but love for the Army," I concluded.

"So, back to square one." His handsome face was bleak. "You're going to hate me for this question." I raised an eyebrow, indicating he should ask it anyway. "Could it be somebody in your organization, your little group?" Before I could hotly deny the possibility, he held up his hand. "Whoa. Remember, you said that feelings were sometimes volatile in the environmental movement."

"Volatile, yes. Violent, no," I protested. "For the most part these are gentle decent people with a real concern for animals, the environment, and their fellow man."

"Granted most are," he argued, "but when emotions run high, things get out of hand. Just look at the right-to-life kooks who bomb abortion clinics and harass the patients, or the nuclear-freeze pickets whose demonstrations sometimes go beyond peaceful picketing."

"Okay," I conceded. "We do get a few fanatics in any movement, but damn it, it doesn't compute. I can buy an environmentalist knocking off General Thorne, but not his wife, and certainly not her groom. I can't see an environmentalist kidnapping my daughter. To what purpose? I'm not looking in that direction."

"Then it's back to LaChance," he said, "and until Ricky comes around, that's a dead end. We have a good idea who the kidnapper is, but we don't know who he's working for."

"Chris, get your cop friend out of bed. See if he knows Morgan, where he lives, where he hangs out. I'd like to get to him before Standish does. I don't have to read him his rights."

Chris studied me. "I've never seen you in such a vicious mood."

"You've never seen me when someone was threatening my family," I retorted. "I'm going to take a shower. Make that call."

THE WATER FLUSHED some of the cobwebs from my brain, but I was so tired that my computer was barely ticking. Standish was right; the circuits were overloaded. Even my concern for Jackie was dulled. I wanted nothing more than to slide between the sheets and sleep for twenty-four hours. "Even twenty-four minutes wouldn't be bad," I muttered as I dressed.

I returned to the office. "Get anything?"

"Morgan lives in the Rockaways near the beach."

"Breezy Point?"

"Right. That cooperative development."

"Just down the road from Fort Tilden?" Chris nodded. "Interesting. If he's got Jackie, where's he keeping her? We eliminated the bunker and it's a little difficult to conceal a teenage girl in your house when you live in a private, protected community like that. So where is she?"

"Abandoned barracks?"

I laughed. "Chris, you're a bloody genius. Maybe I should be your secretary and you the detective."

"No thanks. I like regular hours and regular friends."

"New York's full of empty barracks. Check the Army and give them a story about being a writer doing an article on abandoned Army installations. Wake me in a couple of hours. If our kidnapper calls, I want to talk to him."

My dream turned into a nightmare—flashes of a scared, then a mutilated, then a dead Jackie floated through my mind. I woke, screaming, "No, no, no..." then lurched to the bathroom, dashed cold water on my face, returned, and hunkered down on the end of my bed.

"Why in hell did you come home, Jackie?"

My voice surprised me. Croaking, old, defeated. Where was the optimist who believed everything could be improved by streamlining it?

I looked around my room—a room right out of *House Beautiful*. It didn't satisfy me. My life had turned to ashes. Sinking lower and lower, I stared at the floor; I didn't recognize this depressed woman.

Somebody was going to pay.

Chris knocked on the door. "Abby, telephone. Standish. You awake?" He knocked again, harder.

"Yes," I mumbled. "I'm coming." I slipped into a robe and followed him to the office.

Standish growled. "We found Morgan."

Damn, I thought, I wanted to get to him first. "I want to talk to that bastard."

"Forget it, he's beyond listening. He's a vegetable. A motor patrol found him under the Whitestone Bridge, beaten to a pulp. We're calling it robbery and assault, but it probably wasn't, since his wallet was in his pocket."

I signaled to Chris to get me coffee. My mind raced. Ricky beaten, Morgan beaten; it didn't make sense. What did they have in common? Information? Nothing made sense.

"You still there?" Standish snapped.

"Yes, Standish, I'm worried. These people, whoever they are, are becoming more sinister. At first I thought we were dealing with corporation types, genteel white-collar criminals. Now I'm not so sure. That's two vicious attacks and three murders. Goons. And Jackie. Where is she? Why don't they ask me for something? It's as if she had vanished from the earth."

"How long you been in this business?" Standish asked, a faint sneer in her voice.

"Seven years, but—"

"Mostly genteel, but lucrative cases, eh? Well, lady, join us in the muck. Meet some of the vermin we deal with every day, and, lady, they ain't corporation presidents." She paused. "Sorry, Doyle, I know your kid's got you in a tailspin, but your philosophizing bugs the hell out of me and isn't going to help her. We need facts, hard information. My officers and I are handcuffed by the law, but you aren't."

I wondered what she was driving at. Since she had been with me, she had probably bent more laws than she ever had before or would again. Standish was the epitome of a straight-arrow cop, a direct result of the Knapp Commission—a cop who bent over backward to avoid even the appearance of minor improprieties.

She would shun a free cup of coffee as readily as a thousand-dollar bribe.

She continued. "How much money would you say is at stake in that condo deal?"

"Millions. Why?"

"I don't know. The homosexual bit, the love triangle—seem a little too pat to me. I guess your business sense is rubbing off on me. I think your friend in the hospital is the key."

Ricky. Of course.

With my hand over the mouthpiece, I said, "Chris, find out Ricky's condition. Tell them it's urgent that I speak to him." To Standish, I said, "Where're you going to be for the next couple of hours? I'll get back to you."

"Don't do anything foolish," she admonished. "I'll be in my office."

"I won't," I promised, fingers crossed behind my back. Enough moping, I thought, action is what I need.

Chris hung up and smiled. "He's improving. Still in and out of consciousness, but he's out of danger. They didn't want to say when you could talk to him, but I talked to our man. He says they're so busy they wouldn't notice you were questioning him as long as you stayed inconspicuous."

I gave him a thumbs-up sign. "Great. What's more inconspicuous in a hospital than a doctor?"

Chris laughed. "Maybe I'd better call Maria and tell her to get your bail money ready. I'm sure impersonating a doctor is a felony."

"Only if I operate. See you later."

TWENTY-TWO

Late Wednesday Morning

I ENTERED THE HOSPITAL, wearing a white lab coat with a name tag that read "J. Jones, M.D." A stethoscope dangled around my neck as I assumed a properly harassed expression and strode down the hall toward the intensive care unit.

I stopped at the desk and snapped, "Carter's chart."

Barely glancing at me, the nurse murmured, "Yes, doctor," as she handed me the chart.

Flipping the pages, I headed for Ricky's bed. My guard's eyes widened in surprise. I winked before he could say my name.

Catching himself, he said, "Morning, doctor, I think I'll get a cup of coffee." He whispered, "You're lucky. No doctors have been in yet."

I looked around. No one seemed to be paying any attention to me as I held Ricky's wrist as if I was checking his pulse. "Can you hear me, Ricky?" I whispered.

A tiny slit appeared in the blackness around his right eye. "Abby," he croaked.

I smiled. He was better.

"I . . . I . . ."

I saw it hurt him to talk. "Ricky, just listen. I don't have much time. Squeeze my hand once for yes, twice for no. Okay?" He squeezed once.

"Did you find out who owns LaChance?" Two squeezes. I racked my brain. "Could the information be in the Corps files here in New York?" He opened one eye and squeezed my hand.

"Ah, Dr. Jones, I presume," a voice said quietly from across the bed.

I groaned. I had been so engrossed I hadn't heard Dr. Mulvey approach. He scowled at me and I blushed. "I'm sorry, Dr. Mulvey, but I couldn't think of any other way and it's important. My daughter's been kidnapped and I need information fast."

Dr. Mulvey said, "I'm sorry. You could have asked me. I'm not insensitive." He smiled down at Ricky. "Besides, it looks like your visit has perked him up. He seems more alert. I have two other patients up here that I can tend to first." As a nurse headed for us he raised his voice. "Let me know what you think, Dr. Jones. I'll return in a few minutes."

"Yes, doctor." I smiled. To the nurse I said, "Come back after I've finished." As she left I turned to Ricky. "Hey, this doctor business is great. Everybody jumps."

He tried to smile, but couldn't pull it off.

Suddenly I was aware of an absence of sound except for the wheezing and clicking of the machines. When I glanced behind me, my mind refused to accept what my eyes saw. A man, wearing a surgical

mask, crouched in the doorway. Nurses, cowering behind him, were covered by another masked man who
was waving a sawed-off shotgun. Ignoring me, the
man in the doorway was aiming a pistol at Ricky. Of
course, to him I was just a doctor.

"Step aside, doc," he ordered, his voice muffled,
"and you won't get hurt."

I stopped aside, as he said, and in a smooth discus-
throwing motion, fired the clipboard I was holding in
my left hand. It caught him in the mouth. Dropping
his gun, he raised both hands to his face as blood
spurted between his fingers.

I pounced on the gun and snapped a shot at the
shotgun toter. He dropped it and raced down the hall,
scattering patients and nurses before him. I lunged for
the second man, but he recovered his wits and sped
after his partner.

I sprinted in pursuit, yelling, "Stop or I'll shoot,"
but I couldn't do that, as people surged into the hall,
attracted by the commotion.

"Police officer, let me through," I shouted, pushing bodies out of my way. Angrily, I watched the two
men disappear into a stairwell. "Damn, what kind of
security is this?" I snarled, and kicked a breakfast
cart.

I ran back to the desk and yelled at the nurse, "Call
security. Seal all exits. Call the cops and Detective
Standish." I rattled off Standish's number. "Tell her
Doyle needs her." She looked pointedly at my name
tag. "Snap to it, sister."

Flushing, she started to dial.

Ricky was agitated, trying to sit up, trying to talk, tangling his wires. I grasped his hand and gently pushed him back down. "It's all right; they've gone. They won't try again. I'll take care of you. I'm going to move you so nobody will find you."

Minutes later the area was crowded with blue uniforms from the Nassau County police. Towering above all of them was Standish's reassuring face.

Dr. Mulvey joined me at Ricky's bedside. "I hear you have terrific reflexes."

I forced a smile. "I used to pitch semipro softball. I threw a strike."

After the cops left, Standish joined us. "Doyle, you seem to be a disaster looking for a place to happen. Want to tell me what's going on?"

"As soon as I finish arrangements with the doctor, I'll let you buy me a cup of coffee." Standish shrugged and left, and I turned to Dr. Mulvey. "Is there somewhere in the hospital we could hide him?"

Dr. Mulvey rubbed his chin. "How about the Geriatric Building? I'll get him a private room and remove his name from the records. We'll answer any queries with the information that he's been discharged."

"Fine. I'll provide full-time guards."

We shook hands, and he smiled at me. "Thanks for preventing a real bloodbath, Ms. Doyle. I hope you find your daughter and that she's all right. If you need any help, please call me."

"Thanks, doc. You're a prince."

I found Standish in the cafeteria. "How do you take your coffee?" she asked.

"Black." She'd left the table when suddenly I began to shake. So close. If that clipboard had missed, you'd be a lump of bloody dead protoplasm, I thought. Now I really feared for Jackie's life. Anyone who would send two armed thugs into a hospital had a wanton disregard for human life.

"Stop it," Standish commanded, placing the coffee in front of me. She grasped my shoulder and squeezed hard enough to cause pain. "It's over."

"No...no...it's not," I stammered. "They...still have Jackie." I inhaled, regaining control of my voice and my body. "It's not a game anymore. Whoever has my daughter doesn't have much in common with those clowns who snatched us."

"That reminds me, I checked out some acting companies. It didn't take me long to find Max. The scars were all makeup, but he couldn't disguise the size of those hands. They were hired over the phone, told it was a practical joke. I put the fear of God into him and told him to pass it along to his buddies. What did Carter tell you?"

I sighed "Not much. We were just beginning when all hell broke loose. Dr. Mulvey gave him a shot to calm him down, so it will be a few hours before I can try again."

An officer paused in the doorway, where he scanned the room before heading for our table. "Detective

Standish, we lost the perpetrators. An orderly said they escaped through a basement exit before it could be sealed off. They headed north on Lakeville Road in a white van. He thought it was an old Volkswagen." He looked at me. "Incidentally, we think you hit one of them. We found a smear of blood on the stairway door downstairs."

I shrugged. "Probably blood from his mouth. I hit him with a clipboard."

Standish said, "I'll alert the city hospitals. Will you take care of calling Suffolk County in case they headed that way?" He nodded. "Could you also send me a full report?"

She handed him her card. After he left, she said, "You're lucky Clark and Dombrosky didn't show up."

I managed a weak grin. "That's all I'd need. They'd run me in for making excessive noise in a hospital zone." I sipped some coffee. "By the way, did you ask how they were doing on Ms. Thorne and her groom?"

"Yeh. They think it's tied to the general, so they're sort of waiting to see what we do. They have no leads, unless you count you."

"Do they?"

Her eyes gleamed. "I've done my best to prevent them from counting you—and your accomplice."

"Funny, Standish. You're getting a real sense of humor."

The loudspeaker blared. "Mrs. Doyle, telephone, Main Desk."

"Must be Chris. He's the only one who knows where I am."

Standish followed me to the desk, where an elderly lady handed me the phone.

A voice whispered, "Doyle, how would you like it if I returned your daughter..."

"When?" I interjected.

A guttural laugh. "You didn't let me finish. How would you like it if I returned your daughter—piece by piece?" *Click.*

I dropped the phone on the counter and stumbled toward the door. Standish grabbed my shoulder and spun me around. "Doyle, who was it? What'd he say?"

"He said he'd return my daughter piece by piece."

TWENTY-THREE

Wednesday Afternoon

I DROVE HOME in a daze, not noticing anything and, fortunately, not hitting anything. Once there, I walked straight past Chris to my living-room window, where I stared across the river.

He touched my shoulder. "I heard. Standish phoned me. He called here and insisted on speaking to you, so I thought I'd better give him the hospital number." Chris gripped harder. "Standish said you saved a lot of lives."

"Cancel all my appointments for this week," I said hoarsely. "I don't want to see or talk to anybody except the whispering man. I've got to think this through. I'm tired of being jerked around."

IN MY BEDROOM, I stacked Moody Blues records on the turntable, closed the heavy drapes, and put on my pajamas. I stretched out on the bed in the dark, waiting for the music to take me. I heard the throbbing music, tasted it, submerged myself in it until I came out on the other side with the computer functioning. I pressed the button and let it run.

General Thorne: dead, homosexual, illegal business deals. Lydia Thorne: dead, adulteress. Groom:

dead, knew too much. Ricky: almost beaten to death, second attempt, found out the truth about General Thorne and LaChance. Jackie: kidnapped, weapon to stop me. General Ritter: cleared. Mrs. Thorne the elder: would she kill her own son to avoid a scandal, to protect her granddaughter's career? Morgan: beaten, blackmailer? Kidnapper? Who hired him? Our kidnappers: actors. Whispering man, whispering man, whispering . . .

I jerked upright and checked the clock. Four hours. The room was silent and I felt like a new person. Hungry.

"Chris, are you here?" I yelled.

He entered the kitchen, waving a fistful of messages. "Ready for these?" He peered at me. "You look better."

I grimaced. "Anything important?"

"You mean pertaining to the case at hand?" I nodded. "Various members of the group called offering tea and sympathy, but no concrete information. Standish checked in; she was worried about you. Maybe she's not so bad for a cop." We smiled at each other. "Dr. Mulvey called, suggests you see your friend tomorrow. He's now listed as Mister Mulvey, and is in room 190A in the geriatric area. Dr. Mulvey said try not to do anything that would excite the old gentleman."

Chris hesitated. "Now for the bad news." I looked at him sharply. He held up a placating hand. "No, not about Jackie. The press." I groaned. "It's difficult to keep a shoot-out in the middle of a hospital quiet. They've been on the phone all afternoon. Some are sitting outside. Would you like to hold a press conference?''

I firmly believed in keeping a low profile when I was working on a case, but I wasn't above using the press if it would further my cause. "What do you think?'' I asked Chris.

"Maybe it would be better to ask Maria that question.''

"Right as usual.'' I smiled. "Get her on the phone.''

I sauntered down the hall, where I studied the television screens that viewed the street. *Daily News* and *New York Post* cars were parked on the opposite sides as usual. An ABC television car was also there.

Chris called, "Maria's on the line.''

"Hello, Maria, did Chris explain the situation?''

Maria said, "It doesn't make sense to kidnap your daughter to get you off the case. After all, as soon as they returned her, you'd be free to secure her safety and continue your investigation. I have to conclude either they're amateurs, who hadn't considered all the ramifications of their act, or they kidnapped her to force you to continue your investigation.''

Stunned, I blurted, "You mean the whispering man wants the investigation to continue, but he was afraid I'd conclude it was a personal and sexual thing with the general, not a business problem. Everybody knows I don't handle routine sex cases.''

"Right.''

"Maria, you're brilliant. Give yourself a raise. I'll send Chris home early tonight."

"Should I invite the boys in the band?" Chris asked.

"Yup. I'm going to have a non-press conference."

I paused in the doorway. "Make sure they have a nice drink in hand and are comfortable before I make my entrance. I'd better dress."

I CHOSE CAREFULLY, for casual effect, a maroon velour V-neck over black wool slacks, and deerskin moccasins.

Entering the office, I said to a young woman with a minicam unit perched on her shoulder, "No television, please. This is just a briefing."

Sis Garrity, top crime reporter for the *News*, leaned forward. "You mean off-the-record?"

Arnold of the *Post* glared at her, while Zehr of ABC was busy peering into his hand mirror, checking his teeth and hair, both storebought.

"Yes and no. I might not have anything worth reporting. What can I do for you?"

"The shooting," Zehr snapped. "Why can't we do a little filming, just a background shot or two of you and me talking. You know, the kind of thing I need for my voice-over."

"Maybe later. What about the shooting? I'm sure the police gave you all the facts."

Sis asked, "How did you happen to be there dressed like a doctor?" She was a motherly looking woman with shrewd Irish blue eyes.

"I always wanted to be a surgeon . . ."

"Cut the crap, Abby. You and I go back a long way," Sis said quietly.

"I'm sorry, you're right. I wanted to visit a friend in intensive care, and that was the only way I could get in at that hour."

"The hospital won't give out his name. Will you?" Arnold asked.

"I'm sorry, that would endanger his life."

"Does it have anything to do with your daughter's kidnapping?" Sis asked. I raised my eyebrows. She sighed. "It's difficult to keep a secret when every cop in the city is carrying a photograph of her. A little too much for just a routine missing kid. They didn't put a name to her, but I recognized her. We met last year. Remember?"

The other reporters looked surprised. "Is she your daughter?" they asked.

"This is definitely off-the-record. Sis is right. If you write or televise anything about her kidnapping, you will endanger her life. And don't blame your police sources, they have her listed as missing, possible runaway. I thought the man in the hospital could help me. He couldn't. Now, do you have any questions about the shooting?"

"Did you hit either of the gunmen?"

"I don't think so. The police found some blood, but I think it came from the one I hit with the clipboard."

"Were they after the patient or you?" Sis asked.

I hesitated. "The patient."

But Sis had noted my pause. "Are you sure?"

"Yes. One of them called me 'doc.'"

"Why did you want to talk to the patient?"

Sis and I locked eyes. "For information," I snapped.

"Why did they try to kill the patient?" she probed.

"To keep him from giving me information," I said sarcastically.

"About your daughter, or the Thorne murder?" she asked.

"What's Thorne got to do with this?"

"You tell me, Abby. I know you found General Thorne's body. And knowing you, that would be enough to interest you in the case."

The others watched the two of us, and I tried sending her a telepathic message as I said softly, "I'm only concerned about my daughter at this time. No more questions."

After what seemed an eternity, Sis stood up. "Thanks, Abby. I'm sorry about your daughter. If I can help, let me know."

I smiled at her. I'd always liked Sis. She was a fair reporter. "Nothing, Sis. Keep in touch."

Zehr pleaded, "Could we just have a little film as a cover for the shooting story?"

I glanced at Chris. He nodded. "Okay, Zehr, but make it brief and no trick questions."

After they'd left, I asked Chris how the taping looked.

He rolled his eyes. "I can't stand Zehr, but for once he abided by the ground rules. I'll watch ABC news tonight."

Later that evening I was working on the Erickson project to keep my mind off Jackie when the concealed bell rang. I checked the screen. Mary Ann, surrounded by the rest of the group, was mugging for the camera. I let them in.

Moments later Mary Ann led them into the apartment. "We thought you could use some company. We saw you on TV."

"Go into the office. I'll open a bottle of wine."

Digging behind her on the couch, Mary Ann asked, "Is this where you hide your love letters?"

She brandished a packet and I slapped my forehead. "I completely forgot these. I found them in the Thorne cabin the night the groom was killed." I thumbed the packet. "There must be at least thirty here."

"They're signed with the initial J. Mrs. Thorne the Elder thinks her daughter-in-law's lover was a guy named Jay Farnsworth. Let's see if we can find anything useful."

I doled out the letters, and soon the room was silent except for the rustle of turning pages.

Jill was the first to speak. "How romantic. I wish some man would write me letters like these."

Bob looked uncomfortable. "Slush. Pure slush." He grinned wickedly and said in an artificially deep voice, "Real men don't write love letters."

"I wish he'd dated them," I muttered.

"This may be the last one," Mary Ann said. "He writes, 'I'll see you Thursday. We'll start the New Year off right.'"

"Let me see that." From the tone of the letter I deduced they hadn't seen each other for a while. He also indicated that a drastic change in their relationship was about to occur.

Was she going to become a widow or a divorcée, I wondered, or a corpse?

"I think it's time to look up this Jay Farnsworth."

"How come you didn't get around to him sooner?" Bob asked.

"I was waiting for the LaChance information from Ricky. Thought it would give me a little ammunition, but I can't wait any longer. Farnsworth is beginning to look more and more important."

"Why?" asked Mary Ann. "He was just Lydia's lover."

I smiled. "More than that, Mary Ann. Chris found out he's one of LaChance's top engineers. Now, if we only knew whether or not he worked on the condo project. He could have pressured the general, gotten at him through information provided by Lydia."

Jill interjected, "He might have killed the general, but no way did he kill Lydia. He really loved her."

"Unless they had a lovers' quarrel," interjected Bob. "This guy sounds too good to be true."

"You mean there's no more sensitive male lovers left in the world?" Mary Ann asked with a glint in her eye.

"Enough of this romantic nonsense," I interceded. "Let's break up this meeting. We all need some sleep."

TWENTY-FOUR

Thursday Morning

AS I SCRAMBLED an egg I thought about Jackie. I was inclined to agree with Maria that Jackie was in no immediate danger. Whoever had her was not an ordinary kidnapper. But how did that square with the identification of Morgan in the area about the time she disappeared? Coincidence? Was he working for the kidnapper? And the phone call at the hospital. I had jumped to the conclusion that the shooting and the call were connected, but were they?

Chris dropped some mail on the counter. "I could use some coffee. It's freezing out. Any news?"

"Quiet night. The group came over. Mary Ann found those letters I took from the Thorne cabin. This Farnsworth may be the key to this whole problem." I flipped through the mail. "Checks and bills. Hope they cancel each other out."

"Where'll you find Farnsworth?"

"Try LaChance's office. Get his home address."

A moment later, Chris returned from phoning. "Farnsworth is out of town—Bolivia."

"How long?"

"Since before Christmas."

I frowned. "Doesn't make sense. According to his letters, he was coming home by last Wednesday or Thursday. If he'd heard about her death, he'd definitely return. But if he doesn't know she's dead, he can't be the whispering man." I didn't like it. "Chris, check every airline that flies to Bolivia."

I didn't have to spell it out for him. He nodded. "Where're you going?"

"To see Ricky."

RICKY LOOKED BETTER. The swelling around his eyes had receded. He clutched my hand. "Thanks for yesterday." His voice was low, raspy, but at least understandable.

I smiled. "No problem. I got you in here in the first place. What did you find?"

His eyes shifted away from mine, and he seemed lost in thought. Then he sighed. "LaChance has some connection to the Thorne family."

"Then why would they have to blackmail the general for help? It doesn't make sense. Why didn't the old lady tell me her family owned LaChance?" I stared at Ricky while something gnawed at the back of my mind. I shook my head; my computer was chasing its tail. "Skip that for now. Tell me about the man who did this to you."

"Same two—same two from yesterday."

So, it hadn't been Morgan. The more answers Ricky gave me, the more confused I became. Something was wrong.

I patted his hand. "Get some rest. The gang sends their love."

Until I could satisfactorily dispose of Morgan's part in the case, I was spinning my wheels. I returned to my office and called Standish. "Could I get a look at Morgan's file?"

A long silence. "Where would you like to buy me lunch?"

"My place. One."

As soon as I hung up, Chris came in to report. "Farnsworth flew to Bolivia on December tenth. If he's returned, he hasn't done it on his original round trip ticket."

"He's returned. Get a picture of him. Turn the Sarnoff Agency loose on finding when he returned. Have them check customs." The Sarnoff Agency is a detective firm that I often used to chase down routine information.

"How was Ricky?" Chris asked after he made his call.

"Much better. He connected LaChance and the Thorne family. Interesting. Why didn't Mrs. Thorne mention that when she told me he was an engineer?"

Chris thought about it for a few minutes. "Maybe in that family, women aren't privy to business information."

Remembering Mrs. Thorne's obdurate strength, I couldn't believe she was just one of those sheltered society flowers.

Chris doodled on the pad in front of him. He looked at me. "One thing puzzles me. Farnsworth was Lydia Thorne's lover and an employee of a company probably owned by the Thorne family. How does that make him the whispering man?"

I shrugged. "It doesn't, unless we can prove he returned before New Year's Day. If he did, then he's a prime suspect in General Thorne's murder. At least he had a darn good motive—Lydia. But that still leaves us hanging on Lydia and the groom, to say nothing of Jackie's kidnapping. I can't see any reason for him to snatch her."

Chris slapped his pencil down in exasperation. "Let's stick to industrial cases from now on."

"I didn't select this case. If you recall, it was forced on me because of that stupid beach walk." As I left the room I added, "Remind me not to go next year."

I WAS IN THE KITCHEN making salami sandwiches when Standish arrived.

Dropping a folder on the counter, she grunted, "Here it is, stolen police property."

I laughed at her expression and scanned the file's contents. "What was he doing under the Whitestone Bridge?"

She shrugged. "Notorious homosexual hangout. Stolen-car dump. Take your pick. Maybe just watching the barges going back and forth. The patrol car was looking for stolen cars when they found him."

"Weapon?"

"The proverbial blunt instrument. My guess is a tire iron."

"Why didn't they kill him?"

"Probably thought they had. He's certainly as good as dead. In fact, the doctor doesn't know how he survived. Now he's hooked up to all those machines."

"Did you find out who he worked for?"

Standish muttered, "He worked for the Department of the Army."

"He what?" I looked at her in disbelief.

"Department of the Army," she said firmly. She held up her hand to forestall my questions. "I know it's hard to believe, but I had one of my people double-check and it's true. They didn't want to discuss it. Any time they don't want to answer questions, they just say it's classified." She rolled her eyes. "I even had a friendly call from the police commissioner, suggesting I lay off the Army."

"Well, I don't work for the police commissioner."

Leaving Standish moodily munching her sandwich, Chris and I went to the office. He looked as bewildered as I felt.

"Army," I muttered to myself. To Chris I said, "Call Mrs. Thorne. Tell her I must see her this afternoon." I glanced at my watch. "Around three."

I returned to the kitchen, where Standish was starting on her third sandwich. "It's a wonder you don't weigh three hundred pounds," I chided.

She shrugged. "You have to eat when you get the opportunity." She peered at me. "Now what're you going to do?"

"I wish I knew. What's your next move?"

She shrugged again. "What about your daughter?" she asked. "Our people haven't turned up anything. I don't think she's in the city."

"Nothing here either. I'm inclined to agree with my lawyer. She's safe—a hostage to my staying on the case."

"I hope you're right. See you around."

She picked up the file, tapped it, and looked at me restlessly as if she wanted to add something. Then, with a futile shrug, she left.

I sincerely hoped Standish wasn't getting into trouble by helping me. The faster I could wrap this mess up, the better it would be for all of us.

TWENTY-FIVE

Thursday Afternoon

THE BUTLER ESCORTED me to the solarium. "Mrs. Thorne will be down presently."

Wondering how long "presently" was, I strolled around the room, looking at the Victorian watercolors of seascapes, mostly by Whistler, Collier, Ingram, and Hardy. I studied the Whistler, trying to decide if it was authentic.

A voice behind me said, "He did more than just paint his mother."

Turning, I smiled at Mrs. Thorne. "You're a mind-reader. We tend to think that all the great works of art are hanging in museums."

Her eyes were cold. The white ruffled collar around her throat emphasized her pallor. "Have you found my son's killer?"

"Not yet."

"Then why have you come?"

That's a good question, I thought as my mind rummaged through several possible answers until it hit on an inspired one.

"I wanted to know what you told a man named Morgan when he came to see you."

Her right hand went to her heart. I thought for a moment she was going to faint, but she stiffened. She limped to a chair, sat down, and rang for the butler, who glided into the room. "Tea," she ordered.

I never took my eyes off her. She was good. The grande dame securely in place, disregarding my question, waiting for tea to be served, ignoring me.

Two could play that game. I held my position, staring at her, silently waiting, as if I could wait forever.

The butler carefully placed the tea tray on the table beside her. "Shall I pour?" he asked.

She dismissed him and poured tea into two cups. I picked up mine and added a nauseating amount of sugar since I hate tea, then retreated to my original position and continued to stare at her. If this was to be a battle of wits, I was armed and ready.

"Morgan?" She sat down her tea cup and delicately pressed her lips with a lace handkerchief. "Oh, yes, that ruffian from the city."

I waited, wondering if that was all she was going to say. My eyes strayed to the Whistler. Simpler days.

"More tea?" she asked. I shook my head. "I really don't know what you want from me." There was exasperation in her tone.

I smiled and stared at her hands. Her fingers were pleating and unpleating the handkerchief. Following my gaze, she stopped abruptly, dropping the handkerchief on the floor.

"He was a venal man, a venal man," she said.

I sighed. "Mrs. Thorne, in the interest of time, let me describe your visit with Mr. Morgan. During an investigation he was conducting for the Army, he discovered certain unsavory facts about your son. Since Mr. Morgan felt that his Army pay and his police pension were inadequate, he decided to ask you to supplement his income in return for his suppression of those unsavory facts." I paused. "First, he approached your son, who for some reason, didn't take him seriously. Then he came to you."

I studied her face, but it was blank. She sipped her tea, her head tilted attentively. For all her reaction, I could have been describing a mildly interesting bridge game. I had hoped to shake a response out of her by now because I was running out of ideas.

She gave me a social smile. "More tea?"

I shook my head. "Mrs. Thorne, Morgan has been beaten into a vegetable state. He probably won't live."

"Too bad."

I fired wildly. "Mrs. Thorne, I don't think you hired me to solve your son's murder. I think you hired me for a cover-up."

She rang for the butler. When he arrived, she said, "Show Ms. Doyle out."

After a mocking half bow in her direction, I followed the butler to the door, then asked, "Where are my guards?"

"Madame had them arrested for trespassing."

"I don't believe this," I muttered.

I leaned against the fender of my car and stared at the mansion, wondering if Jackie could be a prisoner in there. I grinned. I couldn't imagine the butler as the whispering man. Down at the bay, cold blue water shimmered in icy sunlight. The bay held no answers either.

I got into my car and started the engine as I continued to study the front of the mansion. Well, Doyle, you could penetrate that bastion of society to look for Jackie, but if you were caught, it would probably mean life in jail.

"And Jackie isn't there," I muttered as I shifted the drive. Not even that old woman would be so arrogant. She didn't need to kidnap Jackie. Mrs. Thorne was already paying me to investigate the murders. Circles within circles.

I headed home, fresh out of ideas.

TWENTY-SIX

Thursday Night

CHRIS PAUSED in his preparation to go home and reported, "Farnsworth returned on December twenty-ninth. There were two LaChance engineers in Bolivia. He used the other man's ticket. He hasn't been at his apartment since he returned. At least no one has seen him."

"Who would he be staying with?"

"He has few friends. He drifted away from them after his wife's death a few years ago. Served as extra man at dinner parties and that sort of thing. That's probably how he met Mrs. Thorne." Chris gathered up the outgoing mail and asked, "Anything I can do for you before I leave?"

"No," I smiled. "I'm planning on a quiet evening."

He paused at the door. "We're going to the theater and dinner. I left numbers where we can be reached."

I ATE A SANDWICH, drank a beer, tried to read a book. I was restless, but didn't know what to do. The phone rang.

"Hello," I said, not waiting for it to go on record.

"I still have your daughter," he whispered.

"Farnsworth, I must see you," I blurted.

A gasp and the click of the phone's dial tone made my heart skip a beat. I slammed the receiver down.

"Fool, fool," I shouted to the empty room. "Oh, Jackie, what have I done?"

Damn my impatience! I'd gambled my daughter's life and lost.

I paced the floor for hours, willing the phone to ring, wondering if I should call Standish. What would I tell her?

At midnight, the concealed bell rang. I stared at the television monitor in disbelief. "Jackie!"

We met in the hall and hugged each other for a long moment. I pulled her inside, where I examined her carefully. "Are you all right? Did he hurt you? I'll kill him if he did."

"I'm fine, really," she said, freeing herself from my embrace. "He's a nice man. He wouldn't hurt anybody."

"Farnsworth?"

She nodded. "He said he needed your help and this was the only way he could get it. Since you worked for Mrs. Thorne, he was afraid she could buy your silence."

"Where is he now?"

"I don't know. He said he'd call you in a while."

"Where did he hold you?"

"That cabin on the farm."

"Of course! It was perfectly safe there after the police finished. Why didn't I think of that?" I ruffled her hair and patted her shoulder, reassuring myself that she was actually home. "Are you hungry or anything?"

"No. He took good care of me. He's not a bad man, Mother. He just didn't know what to do. I told him you'd help him, but he was sure Mrs. Thorne controlled you like she's always controlled everybody else."

I smiled. "She did. She paid the bills." I walked Jackie to the couch. "Tell me all about it—from the beginning."

"You were busy in your office when he called that day, saying he was phoning for Rex, so I left you a note and went outside—"

"Whoa," I interrupted. "How did he know about Rex?"

"Easy. Since the day you went to see Lydia, he'd been following you. He even followed me to Rex's."

"I'm confused. He called before you came here and offered me money to drop my investigation into the general's death."

"I know," she said patiently. "He and Lydia were afraid you'd end up accusing them. They had inside information from the cops and feared you more than them, especially after you ignored their offer and went to work for Mrs. Thorne. When you went to question Lydia, they panicked. They were sure Mrs. Thorne had hired you to frame them."

I raised my eyebrows. "Wouldn't it had been simpler if they'd just leveled with me?"

"They didn't dare. They were confused. Then, when Jay found Lydia's body, he really freaked out."

"Did he kill the groom?"

"Of course not!" She gave me an exasperated look. "He was hiding in the groom's apartment and had sent him to the cabin to retrieve his love letters to Lydia. When the groom didn't return, Jay went to the cabin where he saw you, gun in hand, crouching over the groom's body. He was afraid to approach you. He thought you were the killer."

I shook my head angrily. "If Lydia had talked to me that day, she could have prevented a lot of pain and saved her own life." I cursed my own mistake as well. I should have insisted on talking to her. "Now, tell me all the details about your kidnapping."

"A taxi pulled up, the driver said Rex sent him. It was Jay, but I didn't know that at the time. Later he explained that he had to kidnap me to ensure your help and that nothing would happen to me. I was really frightened. He said that it was the only way he could guarantee that you'd find Lydia's murderer, even though you were working for Mrs. Thorne. He said it would be easier for you if I cooperated with him and didn't give him any trouble."

"Oh, Jackie," I interrupted, "you're so naive. So you went along with him. Didn't you know how frantic I'd be? For all I knew, you were dead or brutalized. He did threaten to send you back in little pieces."

She looked surprised. "I didn't think you'd worry that much. You always act so cool." She giggled. "I told him that piece-by-piece line was a little melodramatic."

I couldn't look at her. My own daughter knew me so little that she thought I would accept her kidnapping with equanimity and continue my life as if she'd never existed. I regretted that I didn't have the time to explore that further now. "We'll discuss my feelings some other time. Continue."

"There's not much more to tell. We played cards and Scrabble. In between he made calls to you. Oh yes, he told me about Lydia, their love for each other, their plans for the future. She was going to divorce the general and marry Jay. They'd been keeping it a secret because they were afraid of the general's mother."

"Even though he works for her," I said sarcastically. Jackie had fallen into the victim syndrome of liking and identifying with her kidnapper.

She frowned at me. "Jay didn't know she was one of the owners until just recently. In fact, he was the engineer who recommended they not do that Jersey condo project. That's when General Thorne talked to him, ordered him to change his report. The general knew about Lydia and Jay and threatened to ruin him and make sure he and Lydia never got together."

I stared at her, trying to determine if she was telling the truth—or rather if Farnsworth was telling the truth through her.

"The general tried to coerce Farnsworth, not the other way around?" I shook my head. "Nothing makes sense. The more I know, the less I understand.

I must talk to Farnsworth before somebody else gets killed.''

"What're you going to do?'' she asked.

"Never mind. You just go to bed. Don't answer the phone or the door. No more adventures for you, young lady.'' I ignored the hurt look in her eyes as I ushered her to her room.

I FRACTURED the speed limit in my drive to the farm, where I drove down the lane until I saw the lights of the cabin. I abandoned my car and walked the rest of the way; I didn't want to blunder into any kind of trap. I wasn't as trusting of Farnsworth as Jackie seemed to be. He might be using her for bait to get to me. I tiptoed around the cabin, peeking into windows. Farnsworth was sitting on the couch, an open book on his lap, his head down. He must have nodded off.

I knocked. He didn't answer. I pushed the door and it swung open. Hesitating on the door sill, I called, "Farnsworth.'' No answer. I walked to the couch, called his name, and shook his shoulder. He slumped sideways. The handle of an ordinary boning knife protruded from his back. The body was still warm. I seem to have a knack for finding warm bodies.

Gun out, I checked the other rooms. Empty. Glancing at the rumpled bed I wondered if that was where Jackie had slept. The Scrabble letters and board were scattered on a card table in the living room. I had a horrible thought as I looked at it; Jackie's fingerprints were undoubtedly all over the place. Short of torching the cabin, there was no way I could expunge all of them. I was sorely tempted to burn the cabin and Farnsworth's body and forget the whole bloody mess. I wanted nothing more than to go home and go to bed—for a week at least.

But I didn't. Now that Farnsworth couldn't talk, I looked for something he might have written down, but someone else had searched before me, carefully and professionally.

I made a cup of instant coffee and sat down at the kitchen table to let my internal computer roll. One of the answers I rejected as too outrageous, wondering if I was losing my powers of observation and concentration.

A thump on the steps startled me and I jumped up, gun pointed at the door as I watched it inch open. My finger tightened on the trigger.

"Friend, Doyle. Put down the gun," Standish growled, holstering her own weapon.

"Great way to get your head blown off. What're you doing here?"

"Your daughter has more sense than you do. She called me. She was worried about you. Where's Farnsworth?"

I led her to the front room and gestured at the body. Swearing steadily, she examined it and turned to look at me with raised eyebrows and a question in those cat's eyes of hers.

I shook my head. "Not me, Standish. I found him like that. I've been sitting here, trying to decide what to do, where to go, who to suspect." I paused, staring at the body. "Everything's all jammed up."

"What happened to that famous computer?"

I smiled. "Even IBMs have breakdowns." I nodded at the body. "Where will the killing end?"

"With your death, my friend," Standish murmured.

I started. "What do you mean?"

"Don't you think they're going to get around to you soon? Especially since you know the answer, but won't share it with anybody. You're the link between all these murders. The common denominator."

"Come on, Standish, you're just trying to scare me, and you're succeeding too."

"But not enough to convince you to level with me. When are you going to tell me everything you know?"

I shrugged. "There's nothing to tell. What are we going to do about this body?"

Standish paced around the living room like a panther for several minutes. Then she sighed. "You and I are going to get into our respective cars and do what we're getting pretty good at—steal away into the night and pretend we've never been here."

I nodded, but before I closed the door behind me, I glanced back at the body. "Jackie said he was a nice man."

Standish yanked open her car door and snarled, "Damn it. I should arrest you for your own protection."

I smiled. "Better not," I reminded her. "Standish, you said I could do things you couldn't. I'll be in touch." I winced as she spun her tires, throwing gravel in my direction. "Temper, temper," I muttered.

I was halfway down the lane when I remembered my unwashed cup with my fingerprints on it sitting in the middle of the kitchen table. "That'll make Clark's day," I said, deciding the case would be finished by the time the Nassau cops could track me down.

TWENTY-SEVEN

Friday Morning

CHRIS SHOOK MY shoulder. "Abby, Abby, wake up."

"Morning already?" I grumbled, opening one eye and glaring up at him. "What are you doing in my room?"

Chris frowned. "Your room? Last time I noticed this was the office. Are you all right?"

I groaned. Then I remembered I'd returned, found Jackie asleep on the living-room couch, left her there, and retired to my office couch to think about Farnsworth and his part in the puzzle.

I sat up. "Hey, Jackie's home."

A broad smile broke out on his face. "That's great, but who took her and how?"

"Farnsworth. He released her last night, wanted my help. I went to see him in the cabin at the farm and guess what—I found him dead."

"Dead? I don't understand."

"*You* don't understand? How do you think *I* feel? Between the time he returned Jackie and when I arrived at the cabin someone stuck a knife in his back. I'm always one step behind, always in time to find a body, never in time to prevent a murder." I rubbed my aching neck. "How am I going to tell Jackie about him? She liked him."

"I'll get you some coffee." Returning, he said, "She's asleep on the couch. How is the prodigal daughter?"

"Fine," I said wryly, "like her mother. It was all a great adventure to her. She didn't think I'd be worried." I shook my head. "Are all kids like that?"

"I wouldn't know. Maria and I have decided to forego the doubtful joys of parenthood."

"Smart. Finish that report for Erickson. I promised it for today. Send it by messenger. I'll check it after I have a little talk with Jackie." I chewed on my lip. "I'm not looking forward to this."

"I don't envy you. Just remember, they're resilient at that age and she didn't really know him well."

I SHOOK JACKIE gently and handed her a cup of coffee when she sat up and eyed me doubtfully.

"You look sad," she said. "Is something wrong?"

I stared out the window at Manhattan. "There's no easy way to tell you this, Jackie. I found Farnsworth dead." Her hand shook, spilling coffee. I took the cup and pulled her close, resting my chin on the top of her head. "I need your help. Tell me everything you can remember, every word he said, everything he did. Can you do that?"

She talked for ten minutes, choking back tears, clutching my hand.

When she finished, I said, "Why don't you take a nice hot shower, make yourself a good breakfast, and try to relax. I have a lot of things to do today. I'll see you later."

While I checked the Erickson report, Chris got us more coffee. "How'd it go with Jackie?"

I shrugged. "She's not a trained investigator but she is observant." I sipped my coffee and stared into space for a few minutes. "I have a feeling, Chris, that we're dealing with two separate entities here. General Thorne's murder is one; the rest of the murders constitute another case altogether, murders of opportunity."

"Isn't that quite a trail of crimes with no solid clues?"

I smiled. "There are clues. Too damn many, too many loose ends. Our kidnapping for one, Ricky's beating for another. If it was to prevent him from giving me the information he had gathered, it was certainly an overreaction. Any investigator could have come up with the same thing in a short time, and what he had to tell me wasn't even that helpful." I fiddled with a silver letter opener. "And why kill the groom? Did he simply get in the way? Blackmail, adultery, chicanery. Worse than a Sidney Sheldon novel."

Chris frowned. "Except that all these people are really dead." He paced around the room. "Another thing. Where was Farnsworth when the general was murdered? Lydia? The groom?"

"Jackie said Farnsworth and Lydia didn't murder the general. They were together that day, probably snug in bed. He was in the cabin the afternoon Lydia led me astray. When she was murdered, he was following me. He found the groom's body after he had sent him to the cabin on an errand. Farnsworth must have felt like a rat in a trap with bodies popping up all over the place. Of course, after the groom's death, the cabin became the safest place around, because as far as the police were concerned, nobody else was at the farm. Let's forget Farnsworth for now."

I stood up and stretched. "You may think I'm crazy," I said, then told Chris my theory. He was stunned. "I see you feel the same way I did when it occurred to me," I said. "I'm going to the hospital. Call Standish in an hour."

RICKY WAS PROPPED UP in bed, looking alert and struggling to read *The Wall Street Journal* with one hand.

"How're you feeling?" I asked after dismissing my guard.

"Much better. Thanks for yesterday." His speech was still slurred. "Doctor says I can go home in a couple weeks." He dropped the paper onto the floor. "Find out anything yet?"

"About what?"

"The general's murder."

I smiled. "I'd almost forgotten the general, there've been so many murders since his."

"Sounds like a maniac on the loose, doesn't it?" he said, shifting his position so he could look at me. I had deliberately picked a spot between his bed and the window so I wouldn't have to look into his eyes. "What's wrong, Abby?"

I sighed. "I think you know, Rick." I moved to the window, where I adjusted the blinds so I could look out and see his reflection in the window at the same time.

I spoke to his reflection. "Think back, Rick, to New Year's Day. You arrived before any of us. It was a beastly day, but you insisted on going for a walk. You even decided *where* we'd walk. You led us inevitably to that bunker. You guided us to the general's body."

I heard Rick's involuntary gasp.

"Everything hinged on my going on that walk and you knew I never missed one. I wondered how the general had stayed dry. It seems obvious now. The road went to the bunker and it hadn't started to rain until seven or after. I called one of the rangers today. He told me you're an avid bird-watcher. You go there often, usually driving your car down the road so you can watch in comfort. Yet on that miserable day, you dragged us through brush and along the beach instead of walking on the road."

I fidgeted with the cord to the blinds. "You knew I'd be so busy protecting our little group that I wouldn't look too closely at any of its individual members. Besides, what possible motive could any of our people have to kill General Thorne? Ostensibly, none of us knew him, but you did, didn't you?"

I laughed. "For a while, I even thought his mother had him killed because he was gay, a disgrace to his uniform, and a possible detriment to his daughter's military career. But General Ritter indicated that Thorne didn't worry too much about that aspect of his life. Independently wealthy people don't generally worry about the ethical or moral questions that bedevil ordinary people. Their attitude is, the public be damned." I cleared my throat. "But there is an old saying: You can never be too thin or too rich. More money, simple old-fashioned greed, seems to have motivated the general's urge to help the LaChance Corporation. It's owned by his family, isn't it?"

"I told you that was possible," he whispered, never taking his eyes off my back.

"Of course," I continued, "you knew someone with my business connections would turn up that information sooner or later. You had to give me something." I smiled. "General Thorne had a kinky habit—he held his business meetings in notorious gay bars, the real raunchy ones, and he had his friend secretly photograph the meetings. General Ritter mentioned this to me, and I had Thorne's apartment searched. They found these." I flipped a package of photos onto his bed and continued to watch his reflection. When he hit the third picture, his head jerked up and he stared at my back, his expression unreadable.

Ricky tried to laugh. "So I'm gay and I didn't want any of you to know."

I shrugged. "Why not? This is New York. We all have some gay friends. Is that why you didn't identify the body?"

He didn't answer.

"Ranger Rick," I muttered. "Everybody admired you, Rick. Always the first on the ramparts in the environmental causes. Stop Westway, save the striped bass, stop offshore dumping, support the Cousteau society, the American Littoral Society, Audubon, the Nature Conservancy. You name it, you were always on the side of the angels. Our Rick who worked on Wall Street and remained pure."

I turned to look him in the eyes. "Or did you?" I glanced at my watch. "Sometime last year, during the course of your work, you discovered a relationship between General Thorne and LaChance. It was your once-in-a-lifetime opportunity to become wealthy or at least free from financial worry. You have a son in a very expensive nursing home. He suffered extensive brain damage in an accident several years ago." Tears were running down his face. I grasped his hand and asked softly, "Do you want to tell me the rest of it, Rick?"

"It was an accident," he whispered. "He scared me."

While he struggled for composure, I said, "Start at the beginning, Rick."

He took a deep breath. "During a routine transaction in our office, I discovered Thorne's connection to LaChance. Later I learned Thorne was pushing for a Corps permit to drain some Jersey wetlands for a major condo and marina project." He brushed away tears. "I—I needed money. The nursing home was raising its rate again, and if I couldn't pay it, they'd send Denny to a state facility. He needed more care every year. I had already embezzled thousands from my own firm.

"I—I tried to blackmail Thorne. He agreed to pay, and we made arrangements to meet for the payoff. I had mentioned our beach walk and he thought it would be amusing to meet in that area early in the morning. He was a strange man." Rick dabbed his eyes.

"What time did you meet?" I asked.

"About seven on the street outside the base. It hadn't started to rain. He got in my car. He teased me, calling it a lovers' tryst. We drove to the bunker and went inside. I asked for my money." His eyes clouded with the painful memory. "He laughed at me. He threatened to snap my scrawny neck, as he put it, and came after me. I—I had a gun. I closed my eyes, the gun went off, he fell down. He was dead...."

"Why did you take a gun with you? Where did you get it? I thought you were anti-guns."

He whispered, "I bought it on the street a couple days before the meeting because I was afraid of him."

"You removed his identification. Then what? How did you dispose of his car and the gun?"

Rick mumbled, "Later I took the bus back, picked up his car, and drove it to a stolen-car dump on Jamaica Bay. It's probably stripped and burned by now. I tossed the gun into the bay."

I shook my head. "Wow, Ricky, you amaze me. Where'd you learn all these things?"

"I read the papers, too."

"Did Thorne really bring the money to pay you off?"

Ricky looked downcast. "No, he never planned on paying me. I—I think he was going to kill me."

I patted his hand. "We'll get you a good lawyer, Rick." Glancing up as Standish entered the room, I asked, "Been here long?"

"Long enough." She looked at Rick. "You have the right to remain silent . . ."

When she finished reading him his rights, she said to me, "You can remove your guard. I'll get a police officer here. I've already cleared it with Nassau County."

To Rick she said, "If it's any consolation, Mr. Carter, we were closing in on you. In spite of Ms. Doyle's protestations, I knew it had to be one of your little group." She cleared her throat. "I'm sorry, truly sorry. From all I've learned about Thorne, he was an unsavory character and a real bully. Oh nuts, what am I doing?"

"Being human," I said. "Can I have a minute alone with Rick?" She nodded. "Wait for me outside," I called after her.

I leaned close to Rick and whispered in case Standish was eavesdropping in the hall. "Who were those men who tried to kill you?"

"I don't know. They took everything I had that mentioned LaChance."

"Did they mention the general?"

"No. They didn't say anything, just started beating on me. They were scared off before they could finish me."

I touched his face gently. "You should have asked me for help, Rick—with your son, with everything. You have a lot of friends. Rest now. I'll talk to you later."

I found Standish leaning against the wall in the corridor. We stared at each other as a nurse hurried by us. Absently, I glanced at my watch. "Rick is only responsible for Thorne's death. What about the rest?"

A sardonic grin creased her face. "Nassau County."

"I beg your pardon?"

"Nassau County. They happened out there," she said gleefully, whipping out her identification card. "Read this—New York City Police Department." She enunciated each word.

"Standish, don't be ridiculous! Remember, you said we were going to solve all the murders."

"Forget it. I've got mine. So long, Doyle, don't call me, I'll call you." She strode down the hall without a backward glance.

I was left with two fleeting thoughts: I'll miss her and what in hell am I going to do with the rest of these murder cases?

TWENTY-EIGHT

Friday Afternoon

AFTER SENDING CHRIS and Jackie on some errands, I locked myself in my office, where I slouched behind my desk, sipping a glass of red wine and brooding. I was ambivalent about my morning's work—pleased that I had solved General Thorne's murder, displeased that I had turned Rick in to Standish. I felt as though I had betrayed him. However, I was reasonably sure he could get off on a self-defense plea if everything worked out the way I anticipated. At least his family circumstances would warrant a sympathy play to the jury. And, I rationalized, Standish had figured it out too.

"Forget Ricky, old girl, you still have three murders to solve," I muttered aloud. Two actually. The groom's murder was an accident. He just got in the murderer's way.

What did Lydia Thorne and Jay Farnsworth have in common? They were lovers. She was married to a Thorne and he worked for a Thorne company. My daughter thought Farnsworth had been a decent man. Mrs. Thorne the elder despised Lydia. I thought Lydia had been a bitch, and why had she tried to harm me? Did she really fear her mother-in-law that much?

Did Lydia really believe the old lady could have so much control over people?

An image of the old lady in the mansion on the hill overlooking the bay came into my mind. Money, reputation, family tradition. What meant the most to Mrs. Thorne?

I kicked my inner computer into gear. In what seemed like seconds I rubbed my eyes and glanced at my watch. Two hours had flown by, but I still needed more information. Abby Doyle, cat burglar, would have to prowl tonight.

I ambled into the living room, where Chris and Jackie were chatting. "How long have you two been back?" I asked.

"An hour," Jackie said. "Chris took me to Rex's. Chris is a pretty good shot."

"Really? And all this time I thought he hated guns."

He shrugged. "I thought her lessons might as well continue."

I patted Jackie lightly on the head as I passed the couch. "I thought you might want to return to California immediately after your experience these past few days."

"Oh, Mother." She smiled at me, a smile that was strangely like my own. "I'm tougher than you think. Maybe you still think of me as that little girl you left behind."

Startled by her perception, I just nodded. "Maybe." I turned to Chris. "I want you to stay here tonight. Have Maria come over too."

He gave me a searching look. "You're near the end?"

"I hope so. Let's catch the news."

Chris pressed a button on the entertainment console, activating a wall panel that slid back to reveal a television set. The promos for the six o'clock news on Channel Four were on. Chuck Scarborough was saying, "... body found on Long Island estate, scene of two other murders this week, identified as a Manhattan construction-company executive." We waited impatiently through three commercials and two other stories before the cameras switched to the porch of the cabin. Detective Clark, mopping at his forehead and stumbling over his words, mumbled, "We have a—a prime suspect. That's—that's all I have to say at this time."

The scene switched to an exterior shot of the elder Mrs. Thorne's mansion while a voice intoned, "Tragedy has struck the Thorne family four times this week with the deaths of General and Mrs. Thorne, their groom, and now, an executive of LaChance Construction, who was reportedly a very close family friend. Mrs. Vivian Thorne, the general's mother, declined to comment. Well known in Long Island and Palm Beach social circles, Mrs. Thorne..." I signaled Chris to turn off the set.

Chris chuckled. "I'll bet Mrs. Thorne loved that close family friend bit."

"This is one time her hired publicists can't protect her, can't keep her name out of the news." I wondered why Standish was sitting on Ricky's arrest. Across the river the lights in the United Nations building were winking out. Snow, just starting to fall, blurred the skyline and caused a halo effect around the Empire State Building's colored lights. Idly, I thought, Friday-night traffic will be a disaster, cars slipping and sliding, careening into each other, causing tie-ups all over the place. New Yorkers panic at the sight of a snowflake.

Leaning my forehead against the cool window-pane, I thought about what was *really* on my mind. If you're wrong, Doyle, if you're wrong... But even making a mistake was better than doing nothing. The killing had to stop. Especially since the only one left to kill was me.

Tentatively, Jackie touched my shoulder. "Mother, is there something I can do for you?"

Turning, I smiled. "Rustle up some of your famous California omelets." After she left, I glanced at Chris. "Is it my imagination or is she becoming less of a California girl?"

"She's all right. After all, she *is* your daughter too." He stood up and stretched. "What are you planning tonight? You have that look in your eye again."

I smiled. "Let's go into the office and talk about it. I don't want to worry Jackie."

TWENTY-NINE

Friday Night

LATER THAT EVENING, Chris, Maria, and Jackie were engrossed in a noisy game of hearts when I slipped out.

Outside, I raised my face to the sky, licked snow off my lips, and sighed. Snow complicates lives. I trudged into the alley. I was brushing snow off the car windshield when it shattered under my hand. Stunned, I thought wildly, I didn't push that hard.

Delayed reaction. I dropped to the ground and rolled behind the car, tugging at my gun. Of course, it had been a shot. I strained to see through the snow, strained to hear when all sound was muffled by snow. I cursed the snow, but it worked both ways; it concealed me too.

I huddled behind the rear passenger-side tire, curling into a small target. Every sense was alert. What direction? Where was the gunman? One? Two? More? Did anybody else hear the shot? No, of course not. I hadn't even heard it.

Damn it, Doyle, you can't stay here like a sitting duck.

He had to be in the alley behind me, between me and the back entrance to the factory. If there was more than one, chances were the other was on the street somewhere. Shivering, I mentally scanned my neighborhood. The factory I lived in, a couple of restaurants, the tennis club, empty lots on the East River, an abandoned railroad right-of-way, decaying railroad bridges towering above the river.

They can pin me down here until I freeze to death, I thought. I have to lure them out in the open. If I can't see them, maybe they can't see me. I poked my head around the tire and stared at the back of the alley. Nothing. Swiveling, I studied the piece of street I could see from my position. I thought I saw a faint shadow, a hint of movement near a parked car across the street.

If I didn't move pretty soon, I'd be too frozen to move at all. I climbed to my knees. Waited, then gingerly I stood up. Waited. So far, so good, nobody had shot at me. I rubbed my knees, praying they'd behave properly when the time came.

Stepping backward, I flattened myself against the wall, barely breathing, waiting for the crack of a shot. I listened. I inched along the wall toward the alley entrance. The dangerous part was ahead. A streetlight faintly illuminated the mouth of the alley. I stopped just short of the sidewalk, clinging to the shadows.

A low cough. Now I was sure. Someone was behind that car across the street. I was also convinced that someone was behind me in the alley.

A flash of light hit the car across the street. The gunman ducked too late. I silently thanked the driver of that passing car as I pegged a shot in the thug's direction and sprinted down the street into the rubble-strewn railroad right-of-way.

A voice from near the car screamed, "The bitch is escaping."

Not looking back or slowing down, I tripped on an ice-covered mound of broken cement. I rolled on the ground, clutching my knees. My pants were torn; blood seeped through my fingers. The pain was so excruciating that I clenched my teeth to keep from screaming. Meanwhile, my mind was yelling at my body, "Get up, get up, run, run, run."

"She's in here someplace. The bitch almost hit me."

"I can't see anything in this snow."

"Jerk, come on, we gotta get her."

Their voices came closer.

Forcing myself to my feet, half running, half limping, I scuttled toward the abandoned railroad bridges. Their shadows towered over the river, beckoning me, offering sanctuary.

I'd passed them a million times; now I wished I had taken time to explore them. Vaguely I recalled a ladder somewhere in the center. My only chance was to get inside of one of them. The two thugs were thrashing around behind me, coming closer.

Suddenly I realized my gun was gone. "I must have dropped it," I muttered, patting my jacket pockets, hoping I had stuck it in one of them as I had fallen. Terrific. Two gunmen and I have no gun.

I scrambled over the jagged lumps of concrete leading to the bridge ladder. So much pain now. My circuits were overloaded; numbness had set in. The outline of the ladder emerged in front of me. Desperately, I leaped and grabbed the bottom rung. My fingers slipped, every muscle shrieking.

"There she is!"

Two shots rang out; one hit the ladder near my left hand. My hand stung so much I almost let go, but I scrambled up the ladder expecting each moment to be my last.

Thoughts tumbled through my mind. My daughter—I'd never get to know her now. I hadn't told her how much I loved her. And Standish would never know what had happened to me. I hadn't told anybody what I was going to do. Yes, I had. Chris. Chris would know.

Cold. Pain. Snow. Panic. What had Standish said? Oh yeah, somebody's going to punch your button out someday. You were right, Standish. The old computer is about to short-circuit.

A chugging sound came down the river, a tugboat pushing a barge. I could barely see its lights, and I wondered if the men on the tug would notice me on the ladder. No, they wouldn't be able to see through this snow. I wished I was on that boat with them, sharing a hot cup of coffee.

A shot, coming from below, zinged off metal wide to my left. Guess they can't see too well, either.

After pulling myself up onto the connecting walkway, I realized some of the boards were rotted out. I peered through the gaps in the floor at the gunmen below. They seemed to be arguing, but I couldn't hear their words, only the tone of their voices. Gasping for breath, I closed my eyes. Blood pounded in my ears and I laid my cheek against the rough wood. The board vibrated. I squinted through one eye. One of them was climbing the ladder.

"This thing ain't too steady," he yelled back to his partner.

In my desperate scramble to the top, I hadn't noticed the ladder was rickety. Sighing, I crawled backward, splinters ripping my bare hands and knees. My left foot nudged the wall of the shack. I pushed but nothing happened. Must not be a door.

Slowly, painfully, I turned around and groped for the doorframe. When I found it, I pushed. It was stuck. I gritted my teeth and shoved really hard. The door creaked open a few inches, just enough so I could squeeze through. It was dark. Something rustled. Rats. Damn, I hate rats, but they were preferable to the two behind me. I was afraid to move away from the door, worried that I might fall through some rotten boards. To come this far and fall to my death would be too ironic.

A crack of light gleamed at the door. He had a flashlight. I edged into a corner where I'd be hidden by the door when he opened it. I waited. What was he doing out there? Then I knew. He was waiting for his partner to join him. Big brave men.

I strained to catch their whispers. The wind rattled the structure. My heart was beating so loudly in my ears that I was sure they could hear it pounding. The light snapped out. I felt rather than saw the door move. Automatically, I pulled out the knife from my neck sheath. Thank God I'd worn it tonight. I bared my teeth. No computer now. Just pure cornered animal. Glimpsing a leg, I slashed at it, feeling the knife blade strike bone.

Screaming, he lunged backward and bumped into his partner, who shoved him aside—too hard. The railing snapped. The screaming didn't stop until his body thudded onto the jagged concrete below.

The other one, cursing vehemently, fired four shots into the room, shooting blindly. He wasn't even close. Clutching my head as the sound slammed against my cardrums, I forced myself to remain still.

"I'm going to kill you," he snarled.

I remained silent.

He turned on the flashlight and shone it in my eyes. I couldn't see his face, just that circle of light with death behind it. It's all over. Good-bye, Jackie. I love you. A shot. This was it.

But no pain. So this is death, I thought, amazed that I didn't feel any different. Slowly, I realized it was dark, and the flashlight was gone. Silence. I pinched my ear and felt the pain.

"I'm not dead," I said aloud.

I wasn't shot, he was. Cautiously, I stood up and kicked his body, my mind refusing to believe my senses.

"Doyle, Doyle, you all right? You up there? Answer me, damn it."

I stuck my head through the doorway, where the wind almost tore it off. Down below, a light played along the structure.

"Standish? Is that you?"

Then I collapsed. Dear God, the cavalry had finally arrived. Standish. And I'd thought she had quit this case.

I tumbled down the ladder and sagged into her arms. She slipped an arm around me and half carried, half dragged me back to the street and pushed me into her car. Vaguely, I heard her calling for an ambulance, the shooting team, and the rest of the backup people.

"You didn't shout a warning," I whispered.

She smiled sardonically. "You just didn't hear it. It was windy and you were in a lot of pain, half-conscious."

I grimaced. "You're right. I couldn't have heard it." I clasped her hand. "Thanks, Standish. You were right."

"About what?"

"That famous computer of mine blowing a fuse. I was a goner if you hadn't come along when you did. I dropped my gun in that lot somewhere."

She patted my hand. "You did pretty well. You survived. Don't worry about your gun. One of our people will find it."

A police car skidded to a stop inches behind Standish's. After she talked to the officers, she returned to her car.

"They'll handle things here while I take you to a hospital. On the way you can fill me in on all the details."

AFTER THE DOCTOR pulled out splinters and bandaged my knees, he insisted that I stay overnight. "No thanks, doc," I said. "Nothing personal. I just don't like hospitals. I'll rest easier in my own bed."

On the way home I asked Standish, "How come you showed up in the nick of time? How come you knew where I was?"

She laughed. "I suspected you'd try something, so I convinced Chris it was in your best interest if he kept me posted on your movements. He called right after you left. Just as I got out of my car, I heard a shot coming from that lot, and being the good cop that I am, I went tearing over there, looking for bad guys and expecting to find your dead body." She glanced at me. "Don't be angry with Chris. If he hadn't called me, you'd be dead."

I sighed. "I'm not angry. I pay him for his intelligence."

Standish followed me into the apartment. Pain throbbed in both knees, my hands, and various other parts of my body. I felt like one giant floor burn. Chris, Maria, and Jackie stared at me, a frozen tableau around a card table, until Jackie leaped up and rushed toward me. She reached for me, but I fended her off gently, wincing from the pain of the sudden movement.

"Mom, what happened to you?"

Mom. She'd called me Mom. I savored the word. No longer was I formally Mother—a breakthrough that meant more than solving the case at that moment.

I smiled. "I'm all right. It looks worse than it is. Standish saved my bacon."

Standish blushed and mumbled, "Anybody got a beer for a tired cop?"

I said, "Be back in a minute. Jackie, come with me."

I took her into my bedroom, guided her to the bed, and sat down beside her, holding her hand tightly in mine.

"I don't really know how to say this, so I'll just begin. Jackie, when I was out there and I thought I was going to die, I realized I have never told you how much I love you." She squeezed my hand. I smiled at her and gently touched her cheek. "My heart broke that day you chose your father. I swore I would never allow myself to be vulnerable to that kind of anguish again. I would always be cool, keep a little distance. Up on that trestle I realized how stupid, even selfish, I had been. I love you. Starting today, let's make a new relationship."

Tears glistened in her eyes as she whispered, "I guess we're a lot alike. When I thought you had abandoned me, I swore I'd never love you, never give you the opportunity to reject me again. I've been thinking about it since you told me what really happened, but I didn't know how to talk to you. When I saw you limp through the door just now with all those bandages, I realized how close I had come to never seeing you again. I love you and I really am proud to be your daughter.''

I blushed, brandished an imaginary cigar in my best Groucho manner, and said, ''Enough of this schmaltz, kiddo. Let's join the party.''

AFTER EVERYBODY had settled down, I told them about my adventures in the railroad lot.

''I have one more thing to do,'' I said when I'd finished. I looked at Chris meaningfully. He nodded his agreement. ''Standish, I need your help. Actually, I need a chauffeur. Will you come?''

''Out of my territory, but as a private citizen, I'd be delighted to drive you. Let's go.''

Jackie leaped up. ''Can I come too?''

''Not this time, duck.'' The childhood nickname slipped out. I smiled as I remembered Jackie as a pudgy two-year-old waddling after me like a duck. I ruffled her hair. ''Why don't you get a little sleep. I'll tell you all about it when we get back.''

THIRTY

Saturday Morning

THE SUN, INCHING above the horizon, illuminated the front of Mrs. Thorne's elegant brick Georgian mansion. Slouched in the car seat, gritting my teeth every time Standish hit a bump, I stared at the house as we neared it.

"Beautiful, isn't it? Stop here a moment."

Standish drummed on the steering wheel. "What are we waiting for?"

I contemplated the house, then turned my head and looked at the bay below. "If I had all this, I'd never want anything more." I sighed. "I wonder why, Standish."

She shrugged. "Ask. Let's get it over with." Standish parked the car and leaned her head back against the seat rest. "I'll catch forty winks. Scream if you need me."

The butler opened the door, unflappable even at this hour. He guided me back to the solarium, almost as if I had been expected. Mrs. Thorne was sitting by the window, framed in the reflection of the rising sun. Whistler's mother backlit on Long Island, I thought.

"Mrs. Thorne," I said softly.

Only her head turned, her eyes piercing as ever. She stared at me. "You have a solution," she said flatly.

My legs ached. Without being invited, I limped to a chair, where I sat down gratefully. "I have a solution."

Stubbornly, she didn't ask, so I told her. "Your hired hands are dead. As you can see, I'm still alive, though a trifle battered." Her sigh of relief was almost palpable. I smiled. "I know who killed your son."

She snorted. "I know that—Lydia and her paramour."

So that was it. "I'm afraid you've made a terrible mistake, Mrs. Thorne. They didn't kill your son."

Her hand went to her throat. Her eyes were shocked. "Then—then who?"

"One of my group, Rick Carter, a stock analyst who found out your son had a connection to LaChance. He tried to blackmail the general when he found out about the Jersey condo project. Your son scared Carter, who says he was trying to defend himself when the gun fired accidentally." I paused, looking for a change of expression, but she just stared at me. "I assume your son had mentioned Carter as someone who was trying to interfere in your condo deal and that's why he was nearly beaten to death."

The butler glided into the room carrying a tray. Coffee this time. Gratefully, I accepted a cup and he left.

"I don't understand what you're saying." Her face was ashen. She looked her age.

"Those men who tried to kill me—LaChance employees, hired goons. Right? You hired them to kill Lydia, Morgan. There was a slip-up on the latter, but just as effective. They were also to do in Farnsworth, the groom, Carter—another miss—and finally me—a big mistake. All for naught. Greed, revenge, greed. You have all this." I waved my hand, encompassing the house, the view, her wealth, her social standing.

But great ladies don't crumble easily. She stiffened. Her tone was icy. "You can't prove anything."

I smiled. "I don't intend to try. It would serve no purpose, only hurt your granddaughter, and she's had enough grief. To tell her that her beloved grandmother had her mother killed...I couldn't do that." She sighed. "But you're not getting off entirely," I added quickly. "First, there's my bill, fifty thousand. Remember, I don't work cheap. Second, you will pay for the best criminal lawyer in the country to defend Rick. And third, you will cancel that condo project."

"Or?"

"I don't make idle threats, Mrs. Thorne." I saw the horrified expression on her face and was congratulating myself on how effective I had been when I realized she was looking beyond me. Glancing in that direction, I saw an erect young woman, who was almost the image of the late Lydia.

"Roxanne—my dear," Mrs. Thorne mumbled, half rising, clutching her heart. "It's—it's not what you think."

"You killed my mother. How could you?" Roxanne Thorne crossed the room, stopped in front of the chair, and stared down at her grandmother. The younger woman's expression was filled with anger, hurt, and disgust.

Mrs. Thorne recoiled. "I did it for you, to protect you and your career," she babbled. "Please, Roxanne, you're all I have left."

Roxanne's shoulders slumped and she lowered her head. Her hand reached toward her grandmother, then she yanked it back, straightened her shoulders, and marched to the doorway. "I don't ever want to see you again or hear from you. You're as dead to me as my mother is."

All I could think of was I certainly would never want Jackie to look at me like that.

Mrs. Thorne rose, crying, "Roxanne, come back, you don't understand, I did it for you..."

She slumped into the chair when she realized her granddaughter was gone. The iron lady was crying silently.

"Good-bye, Mrs. Thorne," I said softly.

STANDISH WAS HUDDLED in the car with the heater going full blast. She glanced up when I opened the door. "You look like a corpse," she said as I got in. "How'd it go?"

"Standish, you're so full of compliments. Let's get out of here." I glanced at the house and shuddered.

"Did she confess?"

"Not exactly, but she will make amends in a way and she'll pay for the rest of her days. At her age there's no point in running her through the criminal-justice system." I stared at the house. "She has her own prison, a gilded one, but still a prison. Her granddaughter accidentally overheard our conversation. Mrs. Thorne has lost the only person she really loved."

Standish grumbled. "I don't like it. She should be brought to trial."

"Spoken like a true cop. What proof do we have? Those two thugs were the only ones who could connect her with the murders and they're beyond testifying." I rubbed my forehead wearily. "I made the best deal I could, Standish. The world is not black and white. It's mostly shades of gray. She's no danger to anyone now, and she's just been sentenced to a life of loneliness and despair." I smiled at Standish. "And remember, you were the one who said these cases belong to Nassau County, so forget them."

She scowled at me. "I can't understand how you can be so forgiving. She almost had you killed."

"But she didn't succeed, and, in a way, she gave me back my daughter. Fair trade. Home, James. I'm going to bed for twenty-four hours!"

EPILOGUE

Several Weeks Later

My "THANK-GOD-IT'S-OVER" party was in full swing. We had a lot to celebrate and we were doing it noisily.

The grand jury hadn't indicted Ricky, ruling that he acted in self-defense. Arthur Kristin, the best criminal attorney in America, had manipulated the press into portraying Ricky as an American folk hero fighting the evils of big business. Even his company had declined to prosecute him for embezzlement.

I could imagine the frustration and anger Mrs. Thorne must have felt as the media painted her son as a venal, frightening man. I had heard that Mrs. Thorne was truly a recluse now, neither going out nor seeing anyone at home. I had also read that Captain Roxanne Thorne had resigned from the Army for medical reasons and was working on some kind of building project in Africa.

LaChance Construction Corporation announced that it was dropping its condo project in New Jersey after concluding it was detrimental to the wetlands. At least they had garnered some favorable publicity while losing millions of dollars.

After I received my fifty-thousand-dollar check, I had anonymously donated ten thousand to the police fund for widows and orphans. I knew Standish couldn't and wouldn't accept money for saving my life.

All and all, I thought as I looked around, it's a great party. Although Ricky was still terribly subdued, we coaxed a smile out of him now and then. I knew he was still worried about his son, but I had plans to help out in that department.

Jackie, who had flown in for the party, took Rick a glass of wine and stayed by his side. I winked at her. My beautiful California girl, my daughter, was growing up.

Mary Ann stood at the window, greedily devouring the Manhattan skyline, and sighed. "It's to die for."

"Don't forget my painting," I said in passing. Ostensibly we were celebrating the environmentalists' victory over LaChance. Chris winked at me and we touched glasses, toasting our secret.

Standish arrived late, surveyed the room, and snarled, "I don't belong in this group of do-gooders."

I hugged her. "Why, Standish, of course you do. We've made you an honorary member. Jill, bring out Standish's membership card."

Jill, holding a large box at arm's length, placed it on the table in front of Standish while the rest of us backed up until we were as far away as possible.

Standish eyed it dubiously, wrinkling her nose, sniffing suspiciously. She unwrapped and opened the box. Then she choked and gagged.

"Dear God, a dead fish! You people are crazy!"
She left it on the table and crossed the room to join us.
Amid much laughter everybody hugged her, shook her
hand, and welcomed her to the club.

I raised my glass. "A toast to the Order of the Dead
Flounder and to our newest member, Margaret Standish, Peg."

In the hubbub, I whispered, "For a cop, Standish,
you aren't half-bad."

"Surrounded by a bunch of amateurs," she
groaned.